"You heard me, Paige. I asked if you'll marry me."

"I don't suppose you'd like to explain why on earth you think it would be a good idea."

Austin frowned. "I thought it would be obvious."

"Maybe you could hit the high spots," Paige suggested hopefully. "Just so we're both clear on what kind of a deal we're talking about. I mean, you wouldn't want me to get the crazy idea that you've fallen madly in love with me the last few days. Would you?"

"That would be a little uncomfortable," Austin agreed.

"So why do you want to—" she hoped he'd miss the tiny quaver in her voice "—marry me?"

WIFE ON APPROVAL
Leigh Michaels

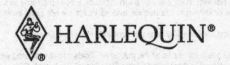

HARLEQUIN®

TORONTO • NEW YORK • LONDON
AMSTERDAM • PARIS • SYDNEY • HAMBURG
STOCKHOLM • ATHENS • TOKYO • MILAN • MADRID
PRAGUE • WARSAW • BUDAPEST • AUCKLAND

ISBN 0-373-03608-6

WIFE ON APPROVAL

First North American Publication 2000.

Copyright © 2000 by Leigh Michaels.

CHAPTER ONE

THE deli had obviously been busy through the lunch hour, for when Paige came in, the serving counter looked as if it had been ravaged by a horde of hungry sailors. She eyed the feeble remains and said, "Just a cup of soup, please."

Looking doubtful, the woman at the counter stirred the contents of the big black soup kettle. "There's not much left but broth, I'm afraid, Ms. McDermott. Now that the lunch rush is past, I'm just starting to restock the sandwich bar, if you'd rather have something heartier. The pastrami is extra good today, the mustard's really hot, and the rye bread is so fresh you can smell it across the room."

Paige's stomach churned at the very idea of the spicy combination. "No, thanks. The soup will do just fine." She carried her thick stoneware mug over to a table where her two business partners were already seated.

Sabrina looked up with a smile and pushed her sandwich wrappings aside to make room for Paige, tipping over her half-full iced tea glass in the process.

Cassie fielded the glass, set it upright without losing a drop, and said without rancor, "Perhaps I was being foolish, Sabrina, to hope that falling in love and settling down would make you just a little less—"

"Clumsy?" Sabrina asked brightly.

"I was going to say, exuberant."

"You don't need to hesitate for fear of hurting my feelings, darling. Caleb doesn't—he says he's going to have his tuxedo tailored out of the stuff they use for bulletproof vests, just in case I trip over the train of my gown and slam into him at the altar.''

"Not only knocking down the groom but pushing all the ushers over like dominoes, I suppose,'' Cassie mused.

Ushers. Paige didn't want to ask who Sabrina's fiancé had ended up asking to accompany him at his wedding; she was afraid she already knew the answer. "Have you ever thought of eloping?'' she asked.

"Frequently,'' Sabrina said dryly. "Especially since my mother got into the act and started coming up with ideas to make my wedding truly unique. But do I sense a little personal tension in that question? You can tell me, Paige. You don't like the bridesmaids' dresses I chose?''

"I wouldn't know,'' Paige said. "I haven't had time to get to the shop to look at them.''

Cassie gathered up the remains of her lunch. "They're absolutely luscious—but have you ever known Sabrina to choose something that's not?''

"Not exactly,'' Paige murmured. "Sabrina's taste is flawless—as long as we're leaving Halloween costumes out of the discussion.''

Sabrina sipped her tea. "You looked great in that costume, and you know it. Besides, Halloween is ancient history. Let's not be distracted from the real news of the day, which is that Paige is half an hour late for a business meeting. I'm not lecturing you, mind, just pointing out that this has never been known to happen before.''

Paige shrugged off the question. "You wouldn't believe the crowd at the supermarket. It's hard enough to try to stock a kitchen from scratch, but having to fight through the aisles in order to do it—''

"Austin Weaver's kitchen?'' Cassie asked.

Paige nodded.

"Tough job," Sabrina sympathized. "I wouldn't have any idea what to buy."

"That's an understatement," Cassie murmured. "When was the last occasion when you spent any time in a kitchen, Sabrina? Other than walking in to refill your coffee cup, I mean."

"That's easy. Just this morning." Sabrina grinned. "Of course, I was hanging new blinds for a client, I wasn't cooking, but—"

"The client should be grateful. And Austin should thank his good fortune that Paige is the one who drew this assignment."

Paige stared at her soup and thought that Austin Weaver was unlikely to do any such thing. Of course, if she had any luck at all, he might not ever know who had arranged the pantry shelves in his new apartment.

"That reminds me." Cassie pulled a bundle of cards from her leather tote bag and flourished them. "I had a great idea last week."

"New business cards?" Paige reached for one. "I thought we had plenty of the old style yet."

"Job cards," Cassie corrected. "To leave after each job is completed." She held up one of the bits of paper and read, "'Your service today was happily provided by Rent-A-Wife. Every working person needs a wife!' And then there's our phone number and a spot to sign, so each client will know exactly who did the errand and how to call for additional service."

"I'm surprised you didn't have individual cards made, with the names already printed," Paige said.

"Should I have? I thought the actual signature would be more personal. Don't you like the idea, Paige?" Cassie sounded downcast. "We're proud of our work, so why not share that fact with our clients?"

"It's a good idea." *It's just the timing that's bad.* Of course, because the cards existed didn't mean she had to use them, Paige thought. She could conveniently forget— at least at certain job sites.... "I have to be going." She pushed her soup aside. "I have Austin's groceries in the van."

"You haven't finished your lunch," Sabrina pointed out. "Not that it was adequate in the first place."

Paige shrugged. "I'll be cooking this afternoon, so I'll no doubt nibble."

"What are you making for the Weavers to eat on their first night in Denver?" Cassie asked casually.

"A chicken and rice casserole. I can leave it in the oven so it'll be ready whenever they arrive."

Cassie looked doubtful. "Will Austin's little girl eat rice? Didn't he say she's five? Sometimes kids that age are awfully picky about their food."

"How should I know what she'll eat?" Too late, Paige heard the sharp edge in her own voice, and she saw Cassie's eyebrows climb. "The request was to leave a meal that will be ready to serve when they arrive this evening. Nobody specified the menu. Besides, if what's-her-name doesn't eat rice, there will be peanut butter in the cupboard."

"So there," Sabrina said under her breath.

Paige tried to smile. At least she'd been successful in making it appear that her irritation concerned five-year-olds in general rather than this one in particular. "Sorry to sound so prickly about it. But it isn't exactly easy to come up with a menu that'll be all right in the oven for hours, in case they're delayed."

"To say nothing of cooking for someone you've never met," Sabrina sympathized.

Paige braced herself. *You're going to have to say it*

sometime, she reminded herself. *You should have told them long before now.*

Cassie was smiling. "If it's the same wonderful casserole you made for my bridal shower, Paige, don't forget to leave one of your new cards. That way Austin will know who to call when he wants another one."

Or he'll know for certain who not to call, Paige thought. *And maybe that's a better idea yet.*

Paige parked her minivan in the loading zone in front of Aspen Towers apartments and eyed the assortment of grocery bags in the back. The small folding cart she always kept in the van was less than adequate for the task, and she wasn't looking forward to making half a dozen trips with it up the service elevator to the topmost apartment in the tower. So she locked the van, bypassed the doorman, who was absorbed in handing a tenant into a taxi, and paused in the open doorway of the building superintendent's office.

The super was talking on the phone, but she made an impatient gesture inviting Paige to step in. While she waited, Paige leaned against the nameplate on the door. Tricia Cade, it proclaimed.

The super turned her chair at an angle and kept talking. Sunlight streaming through the narrow window behind her highlighted her severely cut, platinum-blond hair—a color, Paige knew from the darkness of the woman's eyebrows, that nature had never intended her hair to be. Paige wondered exactly how old she was. Probably only slightly past her mid-thirties, Paige guessed, and it was apparent that Tricia Cade had no intention of ever looking a day older. Perfectly colored hair, sleekly manicured nails, subtle makeup and fashionable clothes were her weapons—and effective ones they were, too.

Beside the super's elegance, Paige felt just a little dowdy. Of course, she'd deliberately chosen her tweed slacks and dark turtleneck for their practicality on a day which involved far more physical work than public appearance; nevertheless she couldn't help feeling inadequate in comparison.

She glanced at her wristwatch. How long was the woman apt to keep her waiting while she talked to what was obviously a friend, not a business contact? By now Paige could have had one load all the way upstairs and be coming back for another. At least, she told herself, with the outdoor temperature hovering at freezing, she didn't have to worry about finding a pool of ice cream in the back of her van. Still, the minutes were ticking by, and a whole afternoon's work remained to be done.

The super obviously saw the restless movement of Paige's hand, for she said into the phone, "Hold on a minute, will you? No, it's not important, it's just my newest tenant's maid needing something." She gave a light laugh at something her friend said and cupped a hand over the mouthpiece.

"That's a common misunderstanding," Paige said. "That Rent-A-Wife is really just a glorified maid service, I mean. Sometimes I wish we'd named it At Your Service instead, because we're actually more like the concierge staff at a big hotel."

The super looked unimpressed. "Is that what you came in to tell me?"

"No, it wasn't." Paige kept her voice level. "I'd like to borrow a cart—a luggage cart or something of the sort—to haul things up to the penthouse."

"I thought the movers did all that earlier in the week."

"I'm sure they'd have taken care of this, too," Paige said sweetly, "if Mr. Weaver had just thought to ship his sugar and coffee and eggs and ice cream along with his furniture, all the way from Atlanta.''

The super waved a hand. ''There's a cart down the hall in the storage closet. The doorman has a key, if the room's locked. You should have asked him instead of bothering me, anyway.'' She put the phone back to her ear and then paused. ''Ice cream? That must mean Mr. Weaver is arriving soon—right?''

''How should I know when to expect him?'' Paige murmured. ''As you so graciously pointed out, I'm only the hired help.''

She regretted the jab as soon as the words were out. She knew better than to make catty remarks to someone in a position to do favors for her, that was sure. *Don't make anyone into an enemy*—it was the first and most basic rule of a service business. What was wrong with her anyway?

She considered apologizing, but decided that the super would be even more annoyed by what she would probably see as yet another interruption, so Paige went in search of the cart instead.

When she let herself into Austin Weaver's apartment a few minutes later, pushing the cartful of grocery bags, she found herself fancying that the spacious rooms held an expectant hush—as if they realized that the new residents would be turning up soon.

She dismissed the notion and hurried toward the kitchen. The logjam at the supermarket had put her well behind schedule, and Tricia Cade hadn't helped a bit. There was still a meal to fix, flowers to arrange, towels to put out, and all the last-minute touches which went so far toward making an impersonal apartment into a home. Touches which all took time. Touches which were particularly important in this case, since Austin Weaver and his daughter Jennifer hadn't yet seen their new residence.

Their first impressions of it could have a dramatic impact on Rent-A-Wife, as well, Paige knew. If Austin Weaver liked the arrangements which had been made for him, Rent-A-Wife would have not only an enthusiastic new client but a good recommendation. If he didn't, the business would be the one to suffer, especially since all three partners had been involved at one stage or another in getting the Weavers settled in Denver so Austin could take on his new job as the chief executive officer of Tanner Electronics.

Cassie had blitzed every real estate agent for miles around till she'd located the best available apartment in the city. Sabrina had whipped the place into shape by organizing the cleaning team and the painters, and then supervising the movers as they arranged Austin Weaver's furniture.

Until today, Paige had managed to stay away from the entire project. But it was only fair that the finishing touches had fallen to her; not only had the other two already done their share, but she was the most domestically inclined of the three, the best cook, and the most detail-oriented. And since she hadn't found just the right occasion to explain to her partners why she'd much rather keep her distance from Austin Weaver, here she was.

With the casserole safely in the oven, Paige took another look at the clock and gave a sigh of relief. It was just midafternoon, so she'd be well out of the way before the Weavers' arrival. She put the flowers, their stems freshly cut, to soak in cold water and went looking for vases. Where would Sabrina have put them? The topmost cabinets in the super-efficient kitchen were entirely empty, and the linen closet yielded nothing more promising. Of course, there was no guarantee Austin owned anything of the sort, she reminded herself.

Paige paused at the doorway of the smaller bedroom and looked in at the sunny yellow carousel horse, the white-painted bookcase crammed with volumes of all sizes and dimensions, the small bed dwarfed by its headboard—an enormous three-story-high dollhouse.

Austin Weaver had a daughter.

She'd known the fact for weeks, of course, since even before he'd actually accepted the job at Tanner Electronics. But it wasn't until Paige was faced with the hard evidence of Jennifer Weaver's existence—the carousel horse, the bookcase, the dollhouse bed—that the child seemed real.

Austin Weaver's daughter. Five years old, and—if the photographs were accurate—a budding beauty.

Paige walked slowly back toward the living room, where a few silver frames were grouped atop a shiny black baby grand piano. The piano was leased, Sabrina had told her, since Austin thought shipping a grand piano cross-country was hardly practical. Paige had had to bite her tongue to keep from saying that she wouldn't be surprised by anything Austin chose to leave behind, and that the only really amazing thing was that he'd collected as much baggage as he had.

She'd settled, instead, for commenting that since Tanner Electronics was paying the bill for his move, and since Caleb Tanner's attitude seemed to be that whatever his new CEO wanted he was to get, regardless of the cost, leaving a baby grand piano behind had been a needless economy.

She paused to straighten the silver frames, which were a fraction of an inch out of line. Austin with an infant in his arms. Austin swinging a toddler over his head. The toddler alone, perched on the carousel horse. A slightly older child, her arms and legs just starting to stretch out of chubby babyhood.

But there was no photograph anywhere she could see of a woman who might be the mother of that toddler...

Paige wondered if that meant the woman's picture was so precious that Austin was carrying it with him instead of shipping it ahead with the rest of his possessions. On the other hand, she thought, there might not be a photograph at all. If it had been a divorce...

Though surely in that case, she mused, wouldn't it would be more likely that the child would have remained with her mother, instead of being placed in the care of a business executive so high-powered and so driven that companies across the country had competed for his services?

Too late, Paige heard the click of a key and then, as the front door swung wide, the soft purring voice of the super. "I'm sure you'll find everything just as you ordered, Mr. Weaver," Tricia Cade said.

Paige froze. *Not yet,* she wanted to say. *I wasn't expecting you till evening, till long after I've gone. You can't come yet.*

Her first instinctive reaction was to dart a look around the apartment, hoping to see an escape route. But the only path from living room to kitchen—and to the service exit where she'd left her belongings—led directly past the front door. For a fleeting instant, she even considered trying to huddle in the shadow of the baby grand piano and hope the coast would clear long enough to let her slip out.

But to be discovered in hiding would only make things worse; she couldn't take the chance. And she had nothing to conceal anyway, Paige reminded herself. No reason to run away.

Maybe it would be just as well to get this first encounter out of the way right now. Even with the super as a witness, it would be a whole lot better to face Austin Weaver now rather than encounter him for the first time in public—maybe even at Sabrina's wedding, when it would feel as if half of Denver would be watching.

Besides, though it wasn't going to be exactly easy, facing him was really no big deal, she told herself. At least it wouldn't be for Paige, since she was forewarned and prepared. Austin would be surprised, no doubt—perhaps even shocked to see her. There would probably be a little uncomfortable small talk. Then they'd both move on—and that would be it.

She tried to take a deep breath to prepare herself, but her chest was so painfully tight that she couldn't seem to draw air into her lungs.

The super pushed the door wide and made an expressive gesture with both hands. "Welcome home! We've all done our very best to make things comfortable for you and your little girl, Mr. Weaver. And I just have to tell you what a darling Jenny is."

Paige hardly recognized the woman's voice; it was a husky, sweet drawl which bore no resemblance to the clipped, irritable tones she'd heard in the office downstairs just a few hours ago.

"My name is Jennifer," said an insistent small voice, and like a magnet Paige's gaze was drawn past the super to the child who was standing just inside the door, her hand tucked into her father's.

Jennifer Weaver was tall for five, Paige thought. She was wearing a red parka with fur trim around the hood. The coat wasn't fastened, and beneath it, Paige could see jeans and sneakers and a sweater with a picture of a cat appliquéd on the front. The little girl's dark hair was tied back in a pair of ponytails, and there was a watchful, almost mulish look on her face.

Tricia chuckled and reached down to ruffle the child's

dark hair. "How formal you are, my dear. But I'm sure we're going to be the greatest of friends."

The child sidestepped the touch and moved away from the door and into the entry hall, where she paused, halfway out of her parka. She made Paige think of a ruby-throated hummingbird—delicate and dainty and full of motion even though at the moment she wasn't going anywhere.

It took a moment before Paige realized what had stopped the child. Jennifer Weaver was staring at her. "Daddy," she said, without taking her gaze off Paige. "Who's that?"

Paige squared her shoulders and stepped forward.

The super turned to stare. "Oh, Ms. McDermott. You're still here." Her voice was full of disdain.

"Just finishing up," Paige said. She was proud of herself; her voice didn't even tremble. She looked beyond Tricia to where Austin Weaver was standing in the shadow of the doorway.

She'd caught just a glimpse of him a few weeks ago, when he'd been interviewing for the job at Tanner Electronics. Even that transitory glance had been enough to make her feel hollow. Still, with the first shock past, the worst was over, she'd told herself.

And now she'd had weeks to get used to the idea of him living in Denver. To ready herself for the inevitable. To get her psyche in shape to meet him once more...

But she had been wrong, she realized as she got her first good look at the man. That single fleeting sight hadn't done a thing to prepare her for coming face-to-face with Austin Weaver. And a whole year of thinking about it wouldn't have done the job, either.

Paige could feel her heart slowing until each beat was like the pounding of a gong, echoing and reverberating through her body. It wasn't fair, she thought. The only change in his face—the only sign that he might be startled—was the slight lift of one dark eyebrow. But then, she thought, Austin Weaver had always been a poker player at heart...

His photographs didn't do him justice, she thought. It wasn't a matter of looks, though indeed the chiseled lines of his face were far more handsome in person than on paper, his dark hair softer-looking, his eyes almost silvery instead of the chilly gray they sometimes appeared in pictures.

What was missing from the photographs was the force of his personality. No camera could begin to capture the magnetic field which seemed to surround him. At a glance, it was apparent that this man not only possessed power, but that he wielded it easily and without hesitation.

It was no wonder the super was practically drooling, Paige thought. Power, money, and good looks all wrapped up in a package and practically delivered to her doorstep...she must have taken one glance and gone straight into vamp mode.

Not that it appeared to be doing her any good. Without turning his head to look at the super, Austin said, "Thank you for bringing us up, Ms. Cade."

"Oh, call me Tricia." The super laid a hand on the sleeve of his leather coat. "It'll be so much more comfortable if you feel you can call on a friend for help."

More comfortable for whom? Paige wanted to ask.

"Now I must show you through the apartment," Tricia coaxed. "Every place has a few eccentricities, you know. Not that there's anything wrong, because we're very careful about maintenance here at Aspen Towers. But I'd be shirking my duties if I didn't show you around."

Paige wanted to applaud. Not only had the super neatly circumvented Austin's attempt to get rid of her, but she'd provided Paige with a line of retreat, as well. The moment the two of them were out of sight, Paige decided, she'd burn a path to the kitchen, jam the flowers into a drinking glass, and get the heck away from Aspen Towers and Austin Weaver....

Coward, she told herself. Running away would only create questions that she didn't want to answer. It would be far better to stay and act casual. As though this sort of encounter happened every day.

Though of course, she reflected, she could always say— and honestly, too—that with her work done there had been no reason to stay longer.

The child dropped her parka in the precise center of the hallway and started toward Paige.

Austin said, "I don't see a coat hook on the floor, Jennifer."

She grinned at him. "But it's all new, so I don't know where it goes."

"Perhaps you should try looking behind that door." He pointed. Then, without checking to see whether she obeyed, he followed the super down the hall.

Jennifer picked up her parka and opened the closet door. "There aren't any hooks my size," she complained and turned to Paige with wide-eyed helplessness.

Unable to resist the appeal in those big brown eyes, Paige took the parka. The soft fur trim tickled her hands as she hung it up. "This is a very pretty coat."

"It's new. I didn't need a thick coat in Atlanta."

"I suppose not."

"I don't like it here. It's cold."

"Yes," Paige said. "It is definitely cold at times. But there are good things about Denver, as well. The mountains, for one, and the wildflowers in the spring—"

"We had a mountain in Georgia. Stone Mountain—with faces carved on it."

"It's true," Paige admitted, "that none of the Rocky Mountains have faces carved on them."

"*Told* you Atlanta's better," Jennifer said, as if there was nothing further to discuss. "What's your name?"

"Paige," she said reluctantly.

"You mean like in a book? That's funny. Are you like a housekeeper?"

"Not exactly. Aren't you going to go look at the apartment?"

Jennifer wrinkled her nose. "She'd just try to pat my head again."

Paige tried to smother a smile. "You don't like Ms. Cade much, do you?"

"She's sticky."

And that, Paige thought, was a pretty good description. Tricia Cade had certainly clung to Austin like caramel on an apple. Paige closed the closet door and started for the kitchen. There were still the flowers to deal with, and then she could escape.

Jennifer dropped into step beside her. "If you're not the housekeeper, who are you?"

"I'm just helping put things in order so you and your father will be comfortable here." Paige took a heavy glass mug from the cabinet. "Will you hang on to this to keep it from upsetting while I arrange the flowers in it?"

From the doorway came a quiet voice. "There you are," Austin said.

Paige's hand slipped and water splashed across the counter. She hadn't heard him come down the hall, but that was partly explained when she realized that he was alone. She wondered how he'd managed to dislodge Tricia so quickly.

"Go explore, Jennifer," he said.

"I don't want to."

"I don't recall asking if you wanted to," Austin said gently. "Your room is just past the front door."

With her lower lip stuck out and her feet dragging, the child went off. "Not my real room," she muttered.

Paige put a shaggy mum into place in the mug.

"So it *is* you," Austin said.

Puzzled, she shot a look at him. Had he not recognized her immediately? Surely she hadn't changed so much that he hadn't known her—though perhaps, since he hadn't been expecting her to reappear in his life...

And yet, he'd almost sounded as if he *had* expected to run into her. *So it is you,* he'd said, as if he was confirming a hunch.

But of course, she thought, both Sabrina and Cassie had talked to him—frequently, in fact—during the weeks they'd been looking for and preparing his apartment. One of them might have mentioned her, and if they'd done so casually, using only her first name—well, it stood to reason that Austin wouldn't have asked pointed questions about a woman who just happened to be named Paige, any more than she'd rushed to volunteer the facts the moment she'd heard he was in line for a job at Tanner. But of course, he would have wondered, and even been watchful.

"It's me." She felt incredibly foolish for not being able to think of anything else to say.

Austin folded his arms across his chest and leaned against the counter. "How have you been?" he asked genially. "And what have you been doing with yourself in the last...let me think, how long has it been, Paige? Six years, I suppose—since our divorce?"

CHAPTER TWO

PAIGE'S voice sounded so taut that Austin wouldn't have been surprised if it had cracked under the strain. "Seven," she said. "It's been almost seven years since the decree was final."

"Has it really?" Deliberately, he kept his tone lazy. "How time does get away."

"When one is having fun, I suppose you mean to say?"

He moved across the kitchen and perched on the edge of a tall stool pulled up to the breakfast bar. Besides being more comfortable than standing, the seat had the advantage of being a safe distance from the counter where Paige was arranging flowers. The downside was that from the breakfast bar he could see three of her—the real one and two hazy blonde reflections in the highly polished stainless-steel doors of the refrigerator.

She didn't look much different, really, than the last time he'd seen her all those years ago. She didn't even look older. Her face was a bit thinner, the fine bone structure more prominent. But perhaps even that change was simply the result of her hairstyle—shorter than he'd ever seen it before, like a fluffy mane that looked as if she could run her fingers through it in the morning and be done with it for all day.

How typical of Paige that would be, he thought, with her almost-Puritan practical streak. While she'd always taken care to look neat and attractive and feminine, Paige had never put much emphasis on the glamorous extras.

He almost laughed at the understatement. In fact, he

21

thought, she'd practically gone out of her way to avoid them...

It seemed to him that outlook of hers hadn't changed in the least, despite the passage of time. Her attitude showed not only in her hairstyle—for flattering though it was, the cut had obviously been chosen for convenience as well as looks—but in her manicure. He watched her slim fingers as she worked with the flowers. Even from across the room, he could see that though her nails were evenly trimmed and buffed to a shine, they were completely innocent of polish.

She'd always avoided bright nail polish, he remembered. He'd told her once it was a shame not to emphasize the delicate grace of her shapely hands by painting her nails red, but she'd simply shaken her head and said brilliant nails were a waste of time, requiring almost constant care and upkeep, with attention to each minuscule chip or scratch.

Yes, he thought, she was the same old Paige....

He drew himself up short. She wasn't the same old Paige, he told himself. If anything, she was probably even more set in her ways than she'd been seven years ago—and he'd be wise to remember it.

She stabbed another stem into the mug. "I should have thought our divorce would be an easy date for you to remember."

Austin frowned. "I don't celebrate it, if that's what you mean."

"Of course not. I'm certainly not saying that our divorce is important enough for you to recall it for its own sake."

She'd gotten better at sarcasm, Austin reflected. More controlled, far more subtle. It flicked him on the raw nevertheless.

"But you can surely remember how old your daughter

is," Paige went on sweetly, "and how long it was before she was born that you met her mother. From there it should be no step at all to recall—"

"How long I'd been free at the time. I see what you mean now. If we've been divorced nearly seven years, and Jennifer's soon going to be six... You're quite right, Paige." He let a congratulatory note creep into his voice. "It *was* very nearly the same time as when you filed for divorce." He saw her tiny, almost-concealed shudder. "What's the matter? Are you jealous because I moved on with my life, and you haven't?"

"Of course I'm not jealous. Your choices have no significance for me. Besides, why would you think I'm stuck in a rut somewhere?"

"Your name, for starters," he said. "The super called you Ms. McDermott—just as you asked of the judge in the divorce petition, when you got tired of being Paige Weaver."

She shrugged. "I made the mistake of giving up my name once, when I married—and it was terribly untidy to get it back. Perhaps the next time around I was just wiser."

"And perhaps," he said curtly, "if you were talking about the truth instead of vague possibilities, you'd be making definite statements instead of subjective ones."

She tilted her chin up. It was a gesture he remembered well; in the old days it had usually meant she knew she was on less-than-solid ground. "All right, so I haven't married again. At least I learned my lesson."

"Meaning what? That I didn't?"

"What other conclusion is there? You got yourself mixed up with a woman while you were on the rebound—"

He picked up an apple from the polished fruit bowl on

the counter and rubbed it against his sleeve. "You're giving yourself quite a little credit there, I see."

"If you're talking about your bad choices, they're not my responsibility."

"No. I mean your assumption that I was on a rebound from you," he said gently, and watched with slightly malicious pleasure as the dart hit her dead center. He bit into the apple with a satisfying crack.

Irritation flared in her big hazel eyes. "Oh, come on, Austin. Even bad marriages—*especially* bad marriages—have aftereffects. People do crazy things after a divorce, no matter how much they wanted to be free."

"You sound as if you're speaking from personal experience. What crazy things did you do?"

"None," she said crisply.

Austin shook his head sadly. "What a shame—to be so repressed that you've forgotten how to let your hair down."

"Attacking me doesn't change the circumstances. It's obvious just from the timing what happened to you—to say nothing of the fact that the relationship obviously wasn't successful. You're here, with your little girl, and her mother is—do you even know where?"

He said wryly, "I don't have a forwarding address, no."

"As I said, at least I learned my lesson."

"Have you." He didn't intend it to be a question. "How is your mother, by the way?"

Paige looked wary. "She's fine."

"Still enjoying her invalidism, I suppose?"

"There's nothing fictional about Mother's disability."

"Only about her dramatic way of coping with it."

"I don't have any idea why you would think I'm interested in your opinions about my mother, Austin."

"Really? That's just about the way I feel concerning your opinions about my life."

She closed her eyes momentarily and he saw a flicker of pain in her face, as if the shaft had gone home.

"It's ironic," he mused, "that the woman who didn't want to be married to me ends up as my hired wife."

"But not for long." Paige wiped off the counter and set the mugful of flowers to one side. "I've left a chicken casserole in the oven for you, and a salad in the refrigerator. Don't worry, neither includes anything but healthy ingredients—the last thing Rent-A-Wife needs is a case of food poisoning laid at our door."

Jennifer bounced down the hall and across the kitchen to fling herself against her father. "It's exactly like my old room! It's just like you promised!"

Over his daughter's head, Austin met Paige's eyes. "Thank you," he said stiffly.

She shrugged. "Not me. Jennifer's room was entirely Sabrina's doing." She washed her hands. "The grocery list you sent has been filled and everything stored away. And now that I've done all I can to make the place ready for you, I'll get out of your way and leave the two of you to settle in."

She brushed past him and picked up her coat from a kitchen chair. "Goodbye, Jennifer." Her voice grew softer. "I hope you'll learn to like Denver despite the cold."

Then she was gone, through a back door Austin hadn't even seen.

Jennifer stared after her. "Why did she go away?"

"Probably because she had other things to do right now."

"Why did she sound like she's never coming back?"

"Perhaps because she doesn't intend to."

"Oh. That must be because she doesn't like you." The child's voice was matter-of-fact.

It wasn't the first time that Jennifer's precocious insight had set Austin back on his heels. Sometimes, he thought, she seemed to be five years old going on thirty—both perceptive and acute.

And even more dead on target than Paige had been, as she'd so curtly diagnosed his weaknesses. Paige, he thought, had missed the mark in a couple of critical areas.

He'd made his share of bad choices, just as she'd deduced, and he wouldn't deny it. But not everything he'd done in the months after their divorce had fallen into the category of things to be regretted.

Take Jennifer, for example. She had been anything but a bad choice.

Why, Paige asked herself miserably, had she let herself be drawn into that insane discussion? Why had she allowed herself to voice her opinions at all? And why had she left herself open to that cutting remark about his lack of interest in what she thought of him?

She could have simply refused to take part in the whole conversation. She could have maintained a cool silence. She could at least have avoided any mention of Jennifer's mother.

But no—she'd had to go behave like a shrew. Not that she didn't have some cause; Austin must have taken up with the woman practically before the ink on the divorce decree was dry, to have a child who was almost six. And it wasn't much comfort to tell herself that many men wouldn't have waited even that long; for all she knew, Austin hadn't waited, either. Though Paige hadn't so much as suspected the existence of another woman at the time, perhaps he had just been very careful, very lucky at keeping a double life under wraps—

"At this rate," she said aloud, "you're going to drive yourself nuts over something that happened years ago and has no significance now. So cut it out."

Paige took a deep breath and tried to clear her mind as she steered the minivan out into rush-hour traffic.

At least, she reminded herself, the first and most difficult encounter was over. And now that Austin knew about her, he'd no doubt be every bit as careful to avoid another run-in as Paige intended to be.

Her cell phone rang, and she took advantage of a red light to dig it out of her leather tote bag.

Sabrina said, "When are you going to be leaving Austin's apartment?"

"I'm headed for home right now. Why?"

"Can you stop by Caleb's house? It's practically on your way."

"My mother will be expecting me."

"Fifteen minutes," Sabrina wheedled. "That's all. I picked up your bridesmaid's dress from the shop this afternoon, because I figured if you were ever going to have time to try it on, it wouldn't be during regular business hours."

Paige tried to smother a sigh. Right now, with every inch of her body still smarting from Austin's words, she didn't want to face either of her partners. She just wanted to go home and...

Not face your mother, she finished. A few minutes' respite from Eileen McDermott's all-observant gaze would be a blessing. In comparison, Sabrina—perceptive as she could be—was downright oblivious. "Sure. I'll be there in a few minutes if traffic cooperates."

"Great. I want to talk to you about something, anyway." Sabrina sounded almost somber.

Paige forgot her own troubles. "It's not Caleb, is it? I mean, you haven't had a fight?"

"Too many to count. It's our favorite pastime." The bounce was back in Sabrina's tone. "But nothing serious. It's my mother that's the problem."

"Again?"

"Are you sure you don't mean *still?* I'll tell you when you get here."

When Paige parked her van in front of Caleb Tanner's three-story Georgian house, Sabrina opened the door to greet her and while she waited for Paige to come up the walk, idly began picking off fragments of loose paint from the siding next to the entrance.

"It'll be a mansion again someday," Paige said as she climbed the crumbling concrete steps. "With your taste and Caleb's money, anything's possible."

"It's just too bad I can't buy enough good weather to work on the exterior in the winter." Sabrina led Paige upstairs to a newly decorated guest room and pulled a garment bag from the closet. "Conversation later," she decreed. "Let's get the important stuff out of the way first."

The dress she displayed was raspberry silk, in an Edwardian style which even included a tiny bustle. It was one of the most beautiful—and impractical—things Paige had ever seen. "Gorgeous," she said as she turned to the mirror, hands holding the neckline in place while Sabrina started to deal with the long row of buttons up the back of the gown. "But don't tell me Cassie's enthusiastic about this color. With that red hair of hers—"

"She's wearing periwinkle blue, but it's styled the same." Sabrina sounded abstracted.

Paige watched her for a moment. "So tell me what your mother's up to."

"She invited my cousin and a friend I haven't seen in at least ten years to be bridesmaids."

"How *thoughtful* of her."

"Wasn't it, though? And that's not the worst of it. She invited them before she bothered to tell me. The first I knew of it was when the old friend called this afternoon to tell me how excited she was about being in my wedding and to ask where she should pick up her dress."

"So what are you going to do? Look around for a couple more ushers to keep the numbers even?"

Sabrina shook her head. "I can't add more bridesmaids, even if I wanted to. Caleb is edgy enough at the very idea of having a formal wedding. I don't dare suggest making an even bigger production out of it. Two bridesmaids, two ushers—that's his absolute limit."

"Then if you're wondering whether I'd mind stepping aside for a substitute in order to keep the peace—"

Paige ran a hand over the sleek heavy silk as she thought about Sabrina's truce with the parents who had once disowned her. It was, she thought, too new and too fragile to risk. And even if Sabrina's mother had veered over the line from helpful to managing...well, she was still Sabrina's mother, after all.

Paige half turned to face her friend and went on, "Surely you know you don't have to ask, Sabrina. I wouldn't be offended, and I'm sure Cassie feels the same. And it wouldn't be too late to have the dresses altered if—"

Sabrina's eyes widened. "I wouldn't dream of asking anything of the sort! You and Cassie are my best friends— if the two of you weren't standing beside me through the ceremony, I wouldn't even feel married."

"It's nice to be appreciated," Paige said lightly, but she felt a tremor deep inside. How lucky she was to have friends like this. "So what are you going to do? Tell them there's been a mix-up, and talk to your mother?"

"You think I haven't already? Their feelings were hurt, and Mother cried and said she was only trying to help." Sabrina sighed. "I'm just afraid of what this desire to be helpful will make her do next." A knock at the door made Sabrina break off, and she went to open it.

Paige turned back and forth in front of the long mirror, admiring the play of light and shadow against the distinct weave of the fabric, only half hearing the murmur of the butler's voice at the door.

Sabrina came back to the mirror, her eyes alight. "Now that's downright lucky," she said. "That I called you over here tonight, I mean. Austin's in town—you must have just missed him at his apartment."

"Actually," Paige began.

"He's downstairs right now, in fact—he stopped by to say hello. It's so sweet of him, I think, to make a courtesy call on his first night in town. Hurry and change out of that dress so you can come down and meet him."

"Sabrina, I—" Paige's throat seemed to swell shut.

"On second thought, don't change." Sabrina grabbed her arm. "Come down just as you are."

Paige said flatly, "I can't."

"Why not? You mean, the dress? It only matters that Caleb not see my wedding gown before the ceremony, you know. The bridesmaids' dresses don't count. Come *on*, Paige—oh, I didn't get nearly all the buttons fastened, did I? Here, turn around and let me finish."

Paige didn't move. "Why are you so anxious for me to meet Austin? And why right now?"

Sabrina's eyes sparkled. "You think I'm trying to fix

you up, don't you?'' She chuckled. ''Darling, I've known you for more than two years, and I've learned the lesson well. I would never dare try to organize anything which even faintly resembled a date for you.''

''That all sounds good,'' Paige said suspiciously, ''but—''

''I just think you should get to know Austin. If Rent-A-Wife is going to keep on taking care of Tanner Electronics' employees, it wouldn't hurt a bit for all three of us to be on speaking terms with the new CEO.''

Paige bit her lip. She could hardly argue with that. And it was a little late to start explaining that she'd gone well past speaking terms with Austin Weaver, all the way to ferocious argument and accusation, earlier this very afternoon—to say nothing of sharing the whole history of her relationship with Austin Weaver while the man himself was waiting just downstairs...

''All right,'' she said finally. ''I'll come down. But I'll have to get into my own clothes first. I can't walk around wearing this elegant dress and my everyday loafers.'' *And I'll take my own sweet time about changing,* Paige told herself. With any luck, Sabrina would mention that Paige was upstairs, and Austin would set a speed record for the door.

''On second thought,'' Sabrina murmured, ''if you're trying to look your best for him, Paige, perhaps I *should* try to organize a date!''

But Paige's luck was cold indeed. Either Sabrina hadn't commented about the friend who'd be coming down in a few minutes, or Austin had seen no acceptable way to excuse himself, for when Paige came down the stairs she could hear the murmur of several voices in the living room.

Among them she had no trouble picking out the low, rich tones of Austin's voice and the high notes of Jennifer's.

Though why, Paige asked herself, should she leap to the conclusion that he'd be uncomfortable enough to run just because she happened to be on the scene?

You'd better get over the idea that you're anything more than incidental to him, she told herself. *And the sooner, the better.*

As the man had said himself this afternoon, he had gone on with his life—and straight on, at that, barely even pausing over the little matter of a divorce. Jennifer's childish soprano ought to be reminder enough of that; even if Paige had once been the most important thing in Austin Weaver's life—which seemed increasingly doubtful, from the evidence at hand—she had long since ceased to be significant.

Just as he was no longer significant to her. She'd made a mistake earlier in the day, allowing herself to put too much importance on the past, allowing herself to become shrill over something which didn't matter at all anymore. Now that she'd realized her error, she could be every bit as indifferent to Austin as he was to her.

She paused in the doorway, taking in the scene at a glance. Austin was seated on the couch, with his back to her and his daughter nestled up against his side.

Knowing she could still walk away, Paige had to force herself to step into the living room.

Sabrina passed a cup to Austin and asked, "You've already been to the apartment, of course? How do you like it?"

"It's very nice. I understand Jennifer has you to thank for the fact that her room looks exactly like the one she had in Atlanta."

"Does it?" Sabrina asked earnestly. "I hoped it would. All the photos you faxed helped, of course."

"But there aren't any right-sized hooks," Jennifer said earnestly. "My size, I mean."

Sabrina frowned. "Oh, dear. I didn't even think of that. It must be because I don't have any little girls of my own."

"I wanted to ask about making the apartment a little more child-friendly," Austin said, "with lower closet rods and coat hooks and shelves that she can reach. Is that the sort of thing Rent-A-Wife does?"

"All the time." As Sabrina settled back with her own coffee cup, her gaze lighted on Paige in the doorway, and she said with a twinkle, "But that kind of job would be Paige's department. Both Cassie and I are hopeless with hammers and drills and screwdrivers, you see. Come on in, Paige, so I can introduce you."

Austin looked over his shoulder, set his cup down, and got to his feet. His expression was bland, Paige saw, showing no recognition, no irritation—and no surprise. He was obviously waiting for her cue, she realized.

She came forward, hand outstretched. Sabrina was watching them fondly, Paige saw, like a matchmaking mama. Annoyed, Paige said under her breath, "Sometimes I wonder what you *are* good at, Sabrina Saunders!"

"Isn't it obvious?" Sabrina said brightly. "Human relations are my specialty."

Before she could go on, Jennifer bounced onto her knees on the couch, leaned over the back toward Paige, and said cheerfully, "Hello. I've forgotten your name, wasn't that silly?"

Paige saw Sabrina's eyebrows soar.

"Do you know what?" the child went on engagingly. "Daddy told me I probably wouldn't see you again."

Paige thought she saw a flicker of annoyance cross Austin's face.

Jennifer's announcement was interesting, Paige thought, in several ways. Because the child had taken her father's statement seriously enough to repeat. Because he'd said it in the first place. Because it so obviously indicated that he intended to avoid Paige. And most of all, because he was clearly put out at his daughter for bringing the matter up.

"Again?" Sabrina asked.

"We've already met," Paige said. She tried to make it sound casual. "I was just leaving the apartment this evening when Mr. Weaver and Jennifer arrived." She offered a hand to the child. "Will you shake hands? I wouldn't dream of patting you on the head, you see."

Jennifer giggled. "She tried again when we were leaving to come over here. It's because my daddy is—"

"Very tired from a long drive," Austin said smoothly. "And it's time for us to go. Thank Ms. Saunders again for your room, Jennifer."

"It's nice," the child said dutifully. "I didn't want to leave my other one, you know, because my mother planned it all for me before she died."

I don't have a forwarding address, Austin had said. Paige had thought he was simply being irreverent. Only in retrospect did she hear pain under the flippant words.

Paige closed her eyes and heard in her brain the echo of every catty comment she'd made in that short conversation with him this afternoon. *The relationship obviously wasn't successful.... People do crazy things after a divorce.... Your bad choices aren't my responsibility.... At least I learned my lesson....*

Her head ached at the memory of every one of those statements—all unfounded, all judgmental, all wrong. Dead wrong.

Why had she never even considered the possibility that Jennifer's mother had died? Why had she so blithely assumed that relationship, too, must have ended in divorce?

Because, Paige accused herself, *he divorced you—and you wanted to believe that he couldn't commit himself to another woman any more than he could to you.*

She'd been determined to believe him incapable of forming a lasting bond with any woman. Even though she'd been faced with the fact that he'd devoted himself to his daughter—evidence that he *was* capable of loyalty— Paige had chosen to consider it unimportant. She'd told herself that to a man, his own little girl was a whole lot different than an adult woman.

She tried to catch his eye, but Austin had focused all his attention on Sabrina, sparing only a nod to Paige before turning toward the door.

"It's time for me to be going, too," Paige heard herself say.

Austin paused, a hesitation so brief and so quickly masked that she found herself wondering if she'd imagined it. But as he held the door for her, she saw a speculative glimmer in his eyes.

She didn't know if she was more annoyed with herself for making a probably rash move, or with him for reading unwarranted meaning into it.

"I do hope I haven't left you with a wrong impression," she said tartly as they stepped off the concrete porch and onto the uneven gravel of the driveway. "I certainly wouldn't want to put myself in the same category as the super at Aspen Towers, coming up with one reason after another to cling to you. I just wanted to say I'm sorry."

"For what?"

"For assuming..." She realized too late that she had an extra—and very interested—listener, and tried to be oblique for the sake of the eavesdropping child. "It never occurred to me... I mean, that it might not have been divorce. Why didn't you bother to correct me, Austin?"

Austin shrugged. "I suppose because it didn't matter."

He obviously wasn't saying that his wife's death didn't matter. So, since it was perfectly clear what he was thinking, Paige told herself irritably, he might as well have just come straight out and said it. *Because it doesn't matter what you think of me.*

She felt awkward. "Of course not," she said quietly. "As long as... I mean, before it comes up again... perhaps we should talk about how to deal with the past."

"Our shared past, you mean? Don't you think it's a bit late for that? You seem to have made your choice already this evening when you referred to me as Mr. Weaver."

"Oh. I suppose so, yes." She paused beside her van, fumbling with her keys. "Anyway, I'm sorry."

Austin walked on toward the Jaguar parked just behind her van, then turned to face her once more. "I don't suppose it's any of my business," he said finally, "but why haven't you told them? Your partners, at least?"

Paige didn't look at him. "Because it wasn't important for them to know."

"Really?" He opened the back door of the car for Jennifer and closed it behind her. "That's very interesting."

"I don't understand what you mean."

"Just this." He took a few steps toward her and leaned against the front fender of his car, arms folded across his chest. "If the fact that we were once married isn't important, Paige, then why on earth are you choosing to make a state secret of *it?*"

CHAPTER THREE

WHEN Paige came in the back door of the little bungalow, pausing to hang the minivan's keys on the hook in the entryway, her mother was in the kitchen, stirring a saucepan of soup on the range.

The flickering light of a muted television set reflected off the chrome frame of Eileen's wheelchair as she turned to face her daughter. "You were in such a hurry to take out the garbage this morning, Paige, that you forgot and left the milk on the top shelf of the refrigerator again. You know I can't reach all the way up there to get it."

Hello, darling. Did you have a good day? You look worried.

I am, Mother. Austin Weaver showed up in my life again. You remember Austin? The man I thought I loved?

Paige smothered a twinge of regret at the thought of a conversation that would probably never happen. It was hard sometimes for her to remember the woman Eileen had once been, before the debilitating effects of her illness had made her so negative, so hard to please.

"I'm sorry to have caused you the inconvenience, Mother." Of course, Paige thought, considering the state of mind she'd been in this morning—knowing she would be spending the day among Austin's possessions and in Austin's new home—it was a wonder she hadn't put the garbage in the refrigerator and the milk on the curb.

"Because of your thoughtlessness, I had to eat my cereal dry."

"I'm sure Linda next door would have been happy to help."

"You know how much I hate asking for favors from anyone." Eileen cleared her throat and went on with a determined note in her voice. "At any rate, it's done now, and there's no point in dwelling on it. You were obviously too eager to get away from here even to notice what you were doing. I can't help wondering, though, what you had on your mind this morning that was so important to you."

So much more important than I am. She didn't say it, but the hint was apparent in Eileen's tone.

Paige picked up a stack of pink message slips from the desk in the corner of the kitchen. "I knew it was going to be a busy day, that's all."

"It must have been. You're quite late."

"I stopped to try on my dress for Sabrina's wedding."

Eileen shook her head. "I wish you weren't going to be part of that circus."

"She's one of my two best friends in the world, Mother. And despite the sheer number of guests who'll be attending, she's planning a simple and very tasteful wedding. There will be no elephants, no lion-tamers, no cotton candy, and no sequined top hats—I promise."

Elaine sniffed. "I notice you didn't bring the dress home. Does that mean you don't want me to see it till it's too late to object?"

"No, it just means I forgot it." Paige flipped through the bits of paper. Most were requests from Rent-A-Wife clients for errands to be run or small jobs to be completed. There shouldn't be anything urgent in this stack; if someone had called with a time-critical job, Eileen would have passed on the message to one of the partners immediately.

Eileen's gaze sharpened. "*Forgot it?* I suppose she

chose it at that lingerie place she likes so well. No doubt you'd be better covered in a swimsuit.''

Paige began sorting the messages into stacks. ''Thanks for taking such good care of the phone calls today, Mom.''

Eileen shrugged. ''What else do I have to occupy myself these days? That pest called again this afternoon.''

''Which pest? Do you mean we're getting prank calls?''

''I suppose you could call it that. I'm talking about Ben Orcutt. The message he left is in there somewhere.''

''I suppose his dishes need washing again.'' Paige sighed. ''Sometimes I wish he hadn't taken Sabrina seriously when she suggested that if he called us more often instead of letting the mess pile up to the ceiling, he'd have visitors on a regular basis.''

''Lately,'' Eileen sniffed, ''he seems to want visitors about three times a week. It would have been more useful, you know, if Sabrina had taught the man to wash his own dishes—but I don't suppose she's practical enough to think of that. You could certainly do without him as a client, now that you have plenty of others.''

''Even if she'd given him lessons, Mother, he'd still be a client. He would just have to come up with another excuse to call. He's lonely, that's all.''

Eileen sniffed. ''Most men are incapable of amusing themselves. To say nothing of actually seeing and taking care of what needs to be done. Your father, for example—''

With the ease of long practice, Paige sidetracked the conversation. ''I can't quite read this sentence. The message from Carol Forbes—what kind of paper does she want me to pick up? Wallpaper?''

''No—an issue of the Denver *Post* that had an article about her nephew.''

''Oh, that's right. I see the date now. If you wouldn't

mind, Mother, we could use a hand with the phones again tomorrow. Cassie's going to try to decorate Christmas trees for four clients tomorrow, and I have to work on arrangements for the staff holiday party at Tanner.'' She set the message slips aside.

Eileen shrugged. ''I certainly don't have anything better to do these days, while I'm sitting at home and waiting for you.''

Paige reminded herself that just because her mother handed her a ticket didn't mean she had to take the guilt trip. ''I thought perhaps you and I could go out this weekend to choose our tree.''

Eileen shrugged. ''Not a lot point in having one. I don't care much about Christmas, anyway, and you're so tired of the holiday by the time it arrives that the whole thing is more effort than it's worth.''

Paige took a long breath. ''It's still Christmas,'' she said firmly. ''We have to do something to celebrate.''

''Go through the motions, you mean.'' Eileen stirred the soup again. ''Or are you feeling a little sentimental?''

''Christmas used to be my favorite holiday.''

''I know,'' Eileen said dryly. ''Back in the old days. You surely aren't thinking about trying to patch things together with Austin, are you, now that he's in town?''

Paige spun around, and her sleeve caught the stack of message slips and sent them whirling into a blizzard of pink snow. ''How did you know—'' She caught herself, but it was too late.

Eileen looked pleased at the reaction. ''I saw a story on the business channel about his new job. You weren't even going to tell me he'd come back to Denver, were you?''

Paige said stiffly, ''I didn't think you'd be particularly interested.''

''How could I not be interested in the man who used

my daughter and then tossed her aside? You're not having any foolish ideas, are you?''

"About wanting him back? Of course not."

"That's good," Eileen said with satisfaction. "Because, of course, it can't be done. And if, instead of rose-colored romantic notions, you're really cherishing any feeble ideas of taking revenge for the way he treated you—well, I don't think you could possibly pull that off, either."

Her mother's blithe assumption that she would fail— that she wasn't attractive enough, feminine enough, or smart enough to succeed—acted on Paige almost like a challenge. So she couldn't possibly win Austin back, could she? And she couldn't possibly figure out a way to get even with him for dumping her? Or, best of all, to accomplish both things at the same time?

Paige was half tempted to take on the dare, not to put Austin in his place but simply to prove that her mother was wrong about her.

Except, of course, she reminded herself, that it would be such a childish thing to do.

Austin had only been inside the offices of Tanner Electronics once before, and that had been just a walk-through to get the lay of the land in order to help him decide whether he wanted to take the job. On that visit Caleb Tanner had been beside him all the while. It was time, he thought, to get a real sense of the people and the business and the surroundings, with no one interpreting or interfering.

So when Austin came into the big glassed-in atrium lobby at the front of the building shortly after lunchtime, he deliberately didn't head directly for the executive wing. He strolled up and down the halls instead, peeking into office cubicles and conference rooms, studying computer screens and listening to discussions.

Tanner was a young firm, small and intimate and suffering from growing pains. That much Austin had known before he'd ever considered associating himself with the business, and it was part of what he'd found so attractive about Caleb Tanner's offer. The challenge of grooming a new company beyond financial success into a position of status intrigued him.

By the time he eventually arrived at Caleb Tanner's corner office, however, Austin found himself frowning. There was no secretary in the outer room—there hadn't been on the day he visited, either, Austin recalled—so he strolled over to the open door of the inner office and knocked softly.

Caleb's back was to the door; he was leaning over the once-gleaming surface of his teak desk, where a no-longer-identifiable electronic device lay in a million pieces, and he was whistling softly as he studied the bits. He turned at Austin's tap, looking startled. "I didn't expect you till Monday," he said, stretching out a hand in warm welcome.

"I got Jennifer enrolled in school this morning, and since she wanted to stay and get started, I thought I might as well come in for a few hours and begin to get acclimated."

"Sabrina said you'd stopped by last night, but I thought you'd take the rest of the week to settle in."

"I intended to," Austin said. "But there's not much settling left to be done. Your Rent-A-Wife team did wonders."

"Not mine," Caleb said. "Or, at least, not *all* mine. I suppose I have to take responsibility for Sabrina, terrifying as the idea is, since I'm marrying her in a couple of weeks. But the other two—''

''An interesting business,'' Austin said. ''Rent-A-Wife, I mean. I wonder what inspired it.''

''It was Paige's idea, I guess. You've met Paige?''

Austin nodded. He wondered what Caleb would say if he told him exactly how long—and how well—he'd known Paige. But he'd closed that door behind him last night. She had made a misleading statement—not a lie, exactly, but a good long way from the whole truth—and by not correcting it then and there, he had in a sense promised that he would continue to be silent.

Besides, he told himself, perhaps that approach was the best one, anyway. Their marriage had been so brief as to be almost nonexistent, and it was so far in the past that dragging it up now would create nothing more than shock value.

''She wanted a more flexible job,'' Caleb said, ''to allow her to take care of her sick mother, so she started up the firm and then the other two partners signed on a few months later. So what do you think of Tanner now that you're on board? The first thing, I guess, is to get an office set up for you. I intended to move out over the weekend so this fancy desk would be waiting for you Monday morning, but you beat me to it.''

Austin couldn't see the whole surface because of the electronic gadgetry scattered over it, but the part he could see was covered with deep scratches. The desk, he thought, was teak, and it had once been a showpiece. Now it looked more like a workbench. ''Thanks, but I wouldn't want to put the chairman of the board out of the space you've grown accustomed to. There are a couple of rooms down the hall that will do fine for me. I'd rather be just a little off the beaten path, anyway—I get more work done that way."

Caleb grinned. "My point exactly. This corner of the building is like dead center of the target, and I've been looking forward to getting out of it. I'll just move out my personal stuff and leave everything else, and you can settle right in to the executive suite and get to work."

On the contrary, Austin thought; moving Caleb out looked like a fairly big job. There were boxes, books and papers—to say nothing of electronic bits and pieces—scattered everywhere in the big room. And the physical clutter might not be the worst of the debris that Caleb had collected, Austin suspected. If the employee who was supposed to occupy the outer office was as inefficient as it appeared, he or she wasn't likely to be a success at working for Austin. "I'd rather hire my own secretary, Caleb," he said firmly. "Fresh start, new loyalties, all that stuff."

Caleb frowned. "What are you talking about? Oh, you thought I was leaving mine for you? I've never had one."

At least, Austin thought, that explained why the outer office was always empty. "I see. Well, even hiring a secretary isn't the first thing on my list. Security is."

Caleb's eyebrows rose. "You mean things like new locks and guards around the building?"

"And some other measures, as well. If you aren't suffering a leakage of information, it's only a matter of time."

"My people are loyal."

"That's beside the point, when a stranger can loiter in the hallway till an office is left empty and then go look at the specs still blinking on the computer screen."

"Industrial spies, you mean? What makes you think they could get by with that kind of behavior?"

"Because I did." Austin's tone was uncompromising. "I've been here for a couple of hours already, walking the halls, and no one challenged me or even asked where I was headed.''

Caleb shrugged. "Maybe everyone recognized you and knew you belonged here now.''

"I think it's more likely they didn't even notice me.'' A flash of movement in the outer office caught his eye, and with sudden suspicion Austin leaped up to check it out. If that room was supposed to be empty, who was listening at the door?

He burst into the outer room and pulled up short at the sight of Paige standing at the desk, arranging a plate where the blotter ought to be.

"What are you doing?'' The question came out more sharply than Austin had intended.

"My job,'' she said crisply. "I'm delivering Caleb's weekly order of cookies. I'd have brought the plate into his office because he prefers to have them while they're still warm, but I heard voices inside so I didn't interrupt.'' Her gaze flicked over him without apparent interest. "You're not wasting any time getting into the part, are you, Austin?''

"What do you mean?''

"Acting bossy. It didn't even occur to me that you'd have taken over Caleb's office quite this fast—but if that's the case, you will tell me where to take the cookies, won't you?''

Caleb, still comfortably stretched out in his chair, called, "Come on in, Paige. I haven't moved just yet, and I need those cookies to give me the strength to pack.''

She picked up the plate.

Austin, feeling just a little embarrassed, followed her across the room, and with nothing better to do at the moment, he let his mind dwell on the twitch of her skirt. Her voice had been sticky-sweet, but the swing of that long skirt showed pure irritation. He'd been right in his assessment last night; her command of sarcasm *had* improved by leaps and bounds...

Though sarcasm was hardly the first thing which that skirt brought to mind, he admitted. It was unfashionably long, leaving just a peek of slim calves and tiny ankles, and he was reasonably sure Paige thought the style was modest and old-fashioned and pretty much all-concealing, or she would never have brought the thing home from the shop. But then, Austin reflected, she'd obviously never got a good look at it from the back. The fine camel-colored wool draped lovingly around her, showing off slim hips and delicately hinting at legs that went on forever.

Or perhaps that was his memory instead, reminding him of the supple body which he had known so well....

He reminded himself abruptly that he had no time for— or interest in—speculating what Paige McDermott looked like these days without her clothes.

But she couldn't have changed too much, he knew, because the sleek, deceptively simple lines of that skirt couldn't lie.

Caleb had unwrapped the plate and was happily inhaling the still-warm scent of chocolate.

"Macadamia nut next week?" Paige asked. "Or would you rather have frosted sugar cookies, in honor of Christmas?"

"More of these would be just fine with me."

Paige was smiling, Austin saw. "You're a creature of habit, Caleb. It's just too bad Sabrina doesn't know the difference between an oven and a dishwasher, or you could have cookies all the time."

"Oh, no," Caleb said comfortably. "That's the real beauty of Rent-A-Wife, you know—I have the best of three worlds."

She laughed at him, ignored Austin, and went away. Austin settled back into his chair and tapped his fingers on the upholstered arm.

Without looking directly at him, Caleb offered the plate of cookies. "I should have doubled my order this week, I suppose."

Austin shook his head. "Not for my sake."

"No cookies? You'll regret that choice, I guarantee it. If you don't mind a bit of advice," Caleb said carefully, "it's not a good idea to get one-third of Rent-A-Wife mad at you by accusing her of being an industrial spy."

"I didn't."

"Well, you may want to hunt her up and make it clear that wasn't your intention, because the last thing you want is to get blacklisted. This business of having a wife on call comes in handy at the strangest times." He bit into a cookie and sighed in contentment. "Of course, if someone had told me a few months back that I'd be saying anything of the sort, I'd have—"

"Caleb, the point is that anyone could walk into that room and listen to your private conversations."

"If they're really private," Caleb offered, "I usually remember to close the door."

"Good idea," Austin said dryly. "But security has to be improved throughout the building. Passes for visitors, identification badges for the staff, a check-in desk in the lobby so guests aren't allowed to wander all over—"

Caleb held up another cookie, obviously savoring the aroma. "The staff won't like it."

"They'll have to get used to it."

"Well, let me think it over."

Austin opened his mouth to point out that the question was his to deal with, now that he was the CEO, not Caleb's. Then he decided not to push the matter at the

moment but let it rest till tomorrow instead. No matter how
much Caleb was looking forward to returning to his en-
gineering duties, the fact remained that for years he'd
been the final authority for every decision at Tanner
Electronics—and it couldn't be easy for him to step out of
that position and turn over a good share of the responsibility to someone else. It would be no surprise if the ad-
justment took him a little time—and Austin could afford
to be flexible.

It was, after all, the main reason he'd come to Tanner.
To be flexible.

What was euphemistically called a cafeteria at Tanner
Electronics was really just a row of vending machines, a
microwave, and a few plastic booths. Paige eyed the of-
ferings without enthusiasm. Candy, chips, and a freezer
case of hot dogs and hamburgers which she'd bet tasted
more like cardboard than real food…

But what Tanner employees ate for lunch wasn't her
problem, of course, and it wasn't the reason she was in the
cafeteria in the first place. She'd been looking for a location for the holiday party she was supposed to be planning—the first Christmas event since Rent-A-Wife had
taken over the social functions of Tanner Electronics—and
it was apparent from a glance that the cafeteria was out of
the question. Not only was it too small, but the atmosphere
was downright depressing.

That left the atrium lobby as the only suitable location,
and in order to pull off the event with any style at all she'd
have to rent tables, chairs, linens, steam tables… And it
was already the first week of December, with the party
less than three weeks away.

Paige stood on the stair landing which overlooked the
lobby, pulled out a notebook, and began to make a list.

The atrium was big enough, no question about that. There would be room not only for tables to seat all of Tanner's employees and their families, but both a gigantic tree and a throne where Santa Claus could chat with the staff's children—

Behind her a door opened and automatically she hugged the railing so it would be easier to pass. But instead of slipping by her, the newcomer paused. "Caleb says I should apologize to you," Austin said.

Paige forced her suddenly stiff muscles to relax. "For what?"

"He thinks that in effect I accused you of eavesdropping, by bursting out of his office the way I did. I happen to believe you have more sense than to think that, or to be offended by it."

"Certainly I have," Paige said.

"Good. I'm glad you agree that no apology is necessary." Austin started to walk on.

"Oh, I didn't go that far," Paige mused. "As soon as you saw me outside Caleb's office you stopped being suspicious—but I'm not sure whether I should be flattered because you trust me not to listen, or annoyed because you think I'm not capable of understanding what I was hearing."

"Oh, for—" He tugged irritably at the cashmere muffler tucked under the collar of his wool overcoat. "You haven't always been this touchy, Paige—or is it just that I didn't notice?"

"And in any case, why should I waste my time looking for silly reasons for you to apologize, when you have plenty of really serious ones?"

"Like what?"

He sounded as if he really expected an answer, and

Paige thought better of the accusation. Did she honestly want him to think that she had nothing better to do than dwell on ancient history? "Nothing new, that's sure," she said and bent her head over her notebook once more. "And no, I haven't always been this touchy—not till you taught me I'd better watch out for myself or be trampled on."

"Don't tell me you're still furious with me for taking that job offer in Philadelphia instead of giving it up and staying here because your mother was ill."

"Oh, no." Paige kept her voice airy. "It's obvious you were right about it being your big chance. I'd have hated for you to miss that—no matter what else you had to give up."

"I did invite you to go with me."

"And no doubt you breathed a big sigh of relief when I refused." She looked up from her notebook. "Tell me, Austin, did you already know that woman when you left Denver?"

"If you mean Jennifer's mother—yes, I already knew her."

"There, you see. It was much better the way it turned out—for both of us."

"No doubt you're right," he said. "You seem to be much happier as a wife in image only. This way you can concentrate on the busywork and the details—you can pretend you're living a normal, everyday married life, and yet you can still avoid any emotional involvement or long-term commitment."

Paige slammed her notebook against the rail. "That's quite the accusation, coming from you!"

"But it's true, isn't it? You couldn't go the distance, Paige. When it came time for a choice—"

"How dare you talk to me about choices, and long-term

commitment, and *going the distance* when you had another woman already waiting in the wings?''

Austin looked down at her for a long moment. ''Thank you for the reminder,'' he said softly. ''About another woman waiting for me, I mean. I told my daughter I'd pick her up after school, and I don't want to be late on her first day. So if you'll excuse me...''

Paige tried not to look after him, but her gaze strayed, following him across the wide atrium to the front doors before—with determination—she turned her back on him and leaned against the railing, two fingers pressed to the pounding vein in her temple.

What was it, she asked herself helplessly, that made her self-destruct whenever Austin came on the scene? Why couldn't she have simply agreed that there was no need for him to apologize and left it at that?

She closed her notebook with a snap, knowing she needed a little cooling-off time before she could think any more about parties, and started down the stairs.

It didn't even occur to her that Austin might not yet be safely out of range until she'd retrieved her heavy coat from the rack at one side of the atrium—it would have to be moved on the day of the party, she noted—and was almost at the main doors.

But he hadn't gone out into the cold wind; he was standing just inside, talking to a petite redhead. Paige didn't see him till it was too late to veer off, so she kept to her course, intending to nod at him and say hello to her partner, but not even pause for more.

Austin didn't give her the opportunity to snub him. Paige was still twenty feet off when he murmured something to the redhead, wrapped his cashmere muffler close about his throat, and went out.

The redhead, unbuttoning her coat as she moved, came

toward Paige. "I'm glad I caught you," Cassie said. "Sabrina wanted me to ask you to do her a favor."

Foreboding tingled through Paige's veins. Sabrina generally had no trouble asking for whatever she wanted; she was probably the most direct and the most verbal of the three of them. So when Sabrina resorted to sending a message instead of candidly asking for what she wanted... "I don't think I want to hear this," she said frankly.

"Oh, it's not so bad. She's having a little dinner party on Saturday night—"

"Isn't that the last thing she needs to be doing, with the wedding just a couple of weeks away?"

"I couldn't agree with you more, but you know Sabrina. She said Austin only starts work here once, and she can't possibly put off welcoming him till after the wedding, so she's invited just a few people..." Cassie shrugged. "Anyway, she wanted me to ask you."

So much for Sabrina's declaration last night that she would never again try to arrange a date for Paige. Her excuse would no doubt be that a dinner party thrown for business reasons was scarcely a date, but the intent was clear enough to Paige. For one thing, Sabrina's "few people" would be mostly couples. Paige and Austin might even be the only singles in the group.

"Ask me? You mean, to come?" Paige heard the nervous squeak in her voice and tried to clear her throat. The idea of attending Austin's welcoming party—especially a small and intimate gathering—was slightly less inviting than sitting in a dentist's chair for a root canal. But she couldn't possibly explain her real reasons to Cassie, and coming up with an acceptable excuse was going to be no picnic. She hated being less than truthful with her partners—and in any case, fibbing was not only distasteful but probably useless; Cassie was likely to see straight through any subterfuge she tried to pull off.

"It's really sweet of Sabrina to think of me," Paige began, "but just because we're partners doesn't mean she has to include me in everything she does. I'd much prefer it if she found someone who works at Tanner and who would actually appreciate the chance to meet the boss socially." She congratulated herself. She hadn't lied, she hadn't explained, she hadn't given herself away. Now all she had to do was stick to her guns while Cassie tried the standard persuasive techniques, and she'd be free and clear.... "Sabrina knows perfectly well I'd rather be in the kitchen than actually at the party, anyway."

Cassie smiled knowingly, and suddenly Paige found herself feeling even more uneasy. *Something,* she told herself, *is way off track here.*

"That's exactly what she thought you'd say," Cassie murmured. "So—since she doesn't need you in the kitchen this time—she told Austin he didn't have to worry about getting a sitter for Jennifer on Saturday night, because she knew someone who would be free."

Paige wanted to swear. She hadn't even suspected there was a trap till it had snapped shut on her. And now what could she say? "We don't provide baby-sitting service," she said feebly. "It's spelled out in Rent-A-Wife's rules. No baby-sitting, no window-washing, no—"

"But she's not a baby," Cassie pointed out. "This really isn't much different from picking her up after school and entertaining her at the orthodontist's office till her appointment, and we do that sort of thing all the time. Of course, if you'd rather not be responsible—"

Paige eagerly opened her mouth to seize on the excuse, and closed it again as soon as she realized how suspiciously innocent Cassie looked at the moment. "What's the alternative?" she asked warily.

Cassie shrugged. "I haven't had the opportunity to meet the young lady," she said. "So I told Sabrina I'd happily watch Jennifer for the evening. Of course, that would leave poor Sabrina short yet another guest at her dinner party— but if I'm taking your place, Paige, you surely can't object to standing in for me. Can you?"

Paige sighed. She might as well surrender; there was certainly no safe route to retreat. Between them, Sabrina and Cassie had seen to that.

"Yes," Cassie mused. "Sabrina said she knew she could count on you—one way or the other. So tell me, Paige—which would you rather do?"

CHAPTER FOUR

PAIGE could hear the doorbell chiming, as she stood outside Austin's apartment on Saturday evening. The sound was rich, sonorous and utterly boring, she thought. It was probably the same two notes as every other doorbell in Aspen Towers, installed when the building was constructed and chosen with no individuality or imagination in mind.

And you, she told herself, *would be a lot easier to please if you were looking forward to this evening.*

She still wasn't certain she'd made the right choice. She didn't regret for a moment missing Sabrina's party. In such a small and intimate gathering, it would be far too easy to slip up. Though Paige wasn't egotistical enough to think that every eye in the place would be on her, the entire group would be watching Austin—the newcomer, the unknown quantity. His attitude toward any of the guests would be noticed. If he was cool toward Paige, people would wonder why. And if—heaven forbid—he wasn't cool...

Paige didn't even want to think about what Sabrina would be like if her matchmaking instincts went into overdrive.

On the other hand, Paige wasn't used to small children. She'd spent just as much time as her partners had in chauffeuring clients' kids to appointments and lessons and practices, of course, but that was different from spending the entire evening entertaining a five-year-old. Not that experience would be much help in this situation, she suspected;

Jennifer Weaver struck her as anything but the average five-year-old.

Paige shifted the considerable weight of the leather tote bag which was slung over one shoulder and raised her finger to the button to ring the bell once more. Before she could press it, the door opened to reveal Austin, in a faultlessly tailored tuxedo. His eyebrows lifted slightly as he surveyed her.

Paige was irritated. "Didn't Sabrina tell you who your baby-sitter was?"

"Of course," he said. "I'm not surprised to see you, Paige. I just didn't expect you to come prepared for a long stay." He stepped back from the door.

Paige felt herself color. She swung the bulky leather bag off her shoulder; she felt like dropping it with a thud in the middle of the hall floor. "On the contrary," she said crisply. "I intend to eliminate the need for a second visit next week by installing Jennifer's hooks and closet rods tonight."

"How very efficient," Austin murmured.

"I thought you'd appreciate the idea." Paige dug through a side pocket of the bag and held out a brass key.

Austin made no move to take it. "What's this?"

"I forgot to return it to the super after I'd finished work the other day, and she wasn't in her office when I came in tonight. I thought perhaps you needed an extra, anyway."

"You'd better hang on to it this evening in case you need to go out."

"What for? I hardly think Jennifer will be in the mood for a stroll—it's freezing out there." She shrugged out of her coat and Austin hung it in the closet.

Small feet pounded down the hall, and a childishly excited voice cried, "Is she here?" Jennifer rounded the corner and skidded into her father. Austin caught her, set her upright, and put his hands on the child's shoulders to restrain her.

"Don't tell me I have a fan," Paige murmured. The whole idea made her feel self-conscious. What on earth had she done—besides *not* pat Jennifer on the head—to earn such an enthusiastic welcome?

"In that case, I won't," Austin said dryly.

Paige listened to his terse instructions about snacks and bedtime, but his voice seemed to come from a distance, for she was still thinking about the cynical note in his voice. Was he annoyed that his daughter had chosen her— of all people—to grow fond of? Maybe even suspicious that Paige might promote that attachment for her own ends?

Eventually Austin put on his wool overcoat and kissed Jennifer goodbye. After he was gone, the child stood quietly in the center of the hallway for a full minute, surveying Paige. Finally, she asked solemnly, "What do babysitters do?"

What kind of question was that? Was the child merely testing the waters to see what she might be able to get by with, or was she leading up to a specific outlandish escapade?

"I suppose it depends on the baby-sitter," Paige said. "And on the child, of course. Tonight, we're going to renovate closets, as you requested—so if you'll unzip my tote bag and sort out the hooks, I'll start putting them up."

Jennifer plopped onto the floor and dragged the heavy bag into her lap. "I've never had a baby-sitter before," she confided. "Why are they called baby-sitters, anyway? I'm not a baby anymore."

Paige felt her jaw drop at the sheer impossibility of the statement. How could the child of a busy, sought-after corporate executive—and single parent—not know all about baby-sitters?

Of course, there was day care; perhaps Jennifer didn't see that as quite the same thing. And she'd probably been in preschool from the time she was out of diapers; that didn't count as baby-sitting, either. But there were still evenings and weekends to account for, and even if Austin wanted to spend every minute of that time with his daughter—a possibility Paige thought less than likely—there must be countless hours when he couldn't possibly have the child with him. What about business trips, late meetings, dinners out with clients? He hadn't gotten to the top of the corporate ladder by working eight-hour days.

You're forgetting her mother, Paige reminded herself. She might have been at home with her daughter; Jennifer had said merely that her mother was dead, and Paige had assumed from the casual tone of the statement that it had happened some time ago. But perhaps that was the reason Austin had wanted a change. If his wife had died just recently—

But that possibility still didn't entirely answer the original question, either. Surely Jennifer's mother would have accompanied him sometimes—and someone would have had to look after Jennifer. A baby-sitter, in other words.

Paige took her cordless drill from the tote bag and removed the few garments from the hall closet so she could see the back wall and judge where to best and most securely place the hooks.

Finally the answer dawned on her. *How hopelessly middle class you are, Paige McDermott,* she told herself, *not to think of it first thing!* "I'll bet you had a nanny. That's almost the same thing as a baby-sitter, only it's all the time."

"Oh." Jennifer sounded disappointed. "Is that all?"

Paige tried to suppress a smile at the disillusionment in the child's voice. "I'm afraid so. Why isn't your nanny here now?"

"She didn't come with us," Jennifer said vaguely. "Daddy said she was tired because I had her ever since my mother died."

Paige could understand that. She wondered if that meant the nanny was retired or simply on vacation.

"Her name was Marliss Howard," Jennifer went on.

"The nanny?"

"No. My mother."

"Oh, I see." *Marliss,* Paige thought. *Marliss Howard.* It didn't ring any bells in her mind; in the whole brief term of their marriage, she didn't recall Austin ever mentioning the name.

Of course, she reminded herself, in those last few confused weeks leading up to the day he'd left Denver—and her—Paige had been preoccupied with the sudden worsening of her mother's illness. He could probably have brought troops of dancing girls home with him and she wouldn't have noticed.

And even if she had known, what could she have done about Marliss Howard? Not much, by then. She couldn't have waved a magic wand and made Eileen whole again—and even if she had left her mother to go with Austin, she would have been preserving an empty shell, not a marriage. It couldn't have lasted long; he'd said almost as much himself when he'd admitted that when he'd left Paige he'd already known Marliss Howard.

Known her well enough that he'd taken her with him. Well enough that, within a year or so, she'd given birth to his child…

Paige tried, without much success, to swallow the bitter

lump in her throat. All that was past, she told herself firmly, and she was only hurting herself by dwelling on it.

She turned her attention back to Jennifer. Wasn't it a bit odd that the child had recited her mother's maiden name, instead of calling her Marliss Weaver? Unless perhaps the woman had been an independent sort. Paige wondered, with a tinge of malice, exactly why Austin had sounded a little grim about the subject of married names. If on top of Paige demanding her own name back as a part of their divorce, his second wife had refused to change hers at all…

Knock off the speculation. It's getting you nowhere.

"That's a very pretty name," Paige said. "Hand me the little black box in the side pocket, will you?"

Jennifer dug into the bag. "You mean your phone?" She held it up as high as she could reach.

The cell phone was an older model, too big for the child's small hands. It slipped out of her grasp as smoothly as if it had been greased and hit the mosaic floor with a dull thud.

Paige started to swear, caught herself, and bit off the words. "I think I'm jinxed," she said.

Jennifer looked stricken. "I didn't mean to drop it." She scrambled after the phone.

"I know you didn't, honey. But the darn thing was just in for repairs a couple of weeks ago because I dropped it into a can of paint." *Because you'd just heard the news that Austin Weaver might be coming back to Denver,* she reflected. "If it has to be fixed again—"

"Paint? Did it get all gunky?" Jennifer pushed a button, and the phone cheeped and glowed. "It still works," she announced.

"That's a relief. Stick it back in the bag, will you? What I really need is the box of drill bits so I can make holes ın the wall for the hooks. Maybe I put it in the pocket on the other side."

Jennifer found the box eventually, and Paige put the first hook into place. As she held out a hand for the second one, however, Jennifer asked, "Do we have to do hooks?"

"I thought you wanted them."

"I do. But right now I'd rather read stories." Her tone was uncompromising. "This is boring and my bottom's cold from sitting on this hard floor."

"Maybe you could get a cushion to sit on. We can read stories later, but right now I need to get this done."

"That," Jennifer announced, "is what my daddy always says."

Paige stopped dead with the drill balanced in one hand and the hook in the other. It didn't surprise her to hear that Austin's work was his top priority. *Some things never change,* she thought. But the sadness in the child's voice caught at her throat.

Just what, Paige asked herself, was so all-fired important about installing hooks and closet rods tonight? Yes, she was busy; until the holiday season was over, she'd have to use a shoehorn to fit a single extra job into her calendar, so it made sense to use her time as efficiently as possible. But was she simply determined to get the work done, or was her single- mindedness really hiding another motivation altogether?

Was she doing her best to stay busy so she could minimize the need to interact with Jennifer? Was she fulfilling her duty to the letter, but at the same time refusing to get any more involved than she absolutely had to?

And if that was so, why was she reluctant to get to know the child? Jennifer wasn't to blame for what had happened between Paige and Austin. It wasn't even the child's fault that Paige had been conned into baby-sitting tonight.

Was she afraid, perhaps, Paige asked herself, that if she got to know Jennifer she wouldn't like her? Or was she afraid that she *would* enjoy Austin's daughter?

Paige put the drill back in her bag and dusted off her hands. "Get up this instant," she said with mock severity. "We can't read stories if you sit there till you're frozen to the floor."

Jennifer grinned, and the sudden glow of happiness in her eyes made Paige's stomach turn over in trepidation. What was she letting herself in for? A whole lot more, she suspected, than a few simple storybooks.

But it was too late to back out, she knew. Too late to have regrets. Too late to avoid getting involved.

She was afraid she was already in over her head.

The drill sounded as loud as a cement saw in the quiet apartment, but Paige had checked, and Jennifer was too sound asleep to notice. The child was curled around her stuffed dolphin, her dark hair tangled on the pillow and her mouth half open, and Paige suspected that even if she pounded holes in the wall right above Jennifer's head, the child wouldn't notice.

Because of the hum of her power screwdriver, Paige didn't hear the front door open, and she dropped a brass screw when Austin spoke. "I thought you'd be done with that by now."

She stooped to retrieve the screw from a crack along the back wall of the closet and cinched it into place. "I might have been if I hadn't read seventy-nine stories instead. At least it felt like that many."

"I forgot to warn you. She's starting to read for herself, but she'll still go through her whole library if she finds a—" He stopped as if he'd thought better of the word he'd intended to use.

"Patsy?" Paige asked gently. "That's all right. I'm sure the experience didn't hurt me. Would you hand me the drill, please?" She placed the bit against the next spot she'd marked and glanced over her shoulder at him. "Thanks for not laughing out loud at the idea that it was me—personally—that she was so eager to see tonight. I didn't anticipate having the reputations of baby-sitters in general depending on me. Has Jennifer honestly never had a sitter before?"

Austin shrugged. "I suppose not. There was always the nanny to depend on, you see."

"And who are you going to depend on now? Or is the nanny just on a well-deserved vacation at the moment?"

Austin draped his overcoat across the back of a chair. "If that's a pleasant way of telling me you didn't enjoy the evening…"

"I didn't expect to," Paige mused. "I'm not particularly comfortable with little kids. But as a matter of fact—"

"She's unusual."

"You can say that again. You've enrolled her at Larrimer Academy?"

Austin nodded. "It came highly recommended."

"It's probably the best in the city. A few of our clients have kids there, and we pick them up for appointments and lessons pretty regularly."

"I'll keep that in mind."

"I wasn't dropping a hint, Austin. Right now we've got just about all the work we can take care of. Hand me another hook, would you?"

"Your business is a success, then." Austin ripped a plastic packet and extracted a pair of screws. "Somehow I never saw you as an entrepreneur, Paige."

"Because I never had the drive," she mused, "or understood the importance of putting business before everything else. Which, of course, is why Rent-A-Wife is such a perfect job for me. I can choose the kind of work I do, the hours are flexible and only as intense as I want to make them—''

''Which explains why you're putting up hooks on Saturday night, I suppose.''

She shrugged. ''It's my choice. Maybe I'll take an afternoon off next week. How was the party?''

''That sounds like a loaded question.''

''Because you think whatever you say will go straight back to Sabrina? That wasn't my intention. I imagine you attend so many of these things that it would take dancing girls jumping out of cakes to get your attention.''

''One dancing girl looks remarkably like another.'' He sounded a little absentminded. ''Paige, I've been thinking about what you said the other day, about me having plenty to apologize for.''

She didn't look at him. Instead, she picked up a few of the coats she'd piled on a living room chair and started hanging them back in the closet. ''Forget it. I was annoyed with you, and that just popped out.''

''You don't want to be more specific?''

''Not particularly. It's water over the dam, anyway.''

''You used to think I owed you something, Paige. You said as much, when you tried to blackmail me into staying in Denver because your mother was ill.''

''That wasn't blackmail,'' she said irritably. ''You'd promised to love and honor—''

''You, Paige—but not the dragon on wheels. And don't forget you'd made the same promise.''

Paige's annoyance died away, replaced by a profound tiredness. No matter what she said, he wouldn't understand; he was incapable. ''It's pointless to talk about this now, you know. Our marriage couldn't have worked, no matter what—it was only a matter of time before it broke up. So there's no value in dwelling on what happened."

"Still, you have a point," he mused. "About owing you, I mean. You worked in that department store—in a job you hated—so we could live on your salary while I got established."

She would never forget coming home from long hours on the sales floor, with feet so tired and achy she could hardly stand. But she wasn't the only one. "You were working, too," she pointed out. "And going to school at the same time."

"We were both making an investment, of a sort," Austin said thoughtfully.

"In a future that never happened." Paige heard the tinge of bitterness in her voice and forced herself to smile, trying to cover up the hurt. "Anyway, as I look back on it, the department store wasn't too bad. I got all kinds of discounts."

He looked faintly interested. "On things like china, as I recall. Do you still have all those dishes you bought at such a bargain when we got married?"

Paige bristled a little. "Yes, I kept the china. Just because it was a discontinued pattern didn't mean it wasn't pretty." *Even though, because it holds memories of you, I felt like smashing every last piece of it.*

"Even though we had trouble some weeks putting food on the plates," he said dryly, "at least we had pretty plates. That's really not the kind of thing I meant, however. Investments should pay dividends."

Was he proposing to pay her? To offer her money in order to soothe his conscience?

To have their life together reduced to financial terms left Paige cold. Everything she had done—every minute she'd worked, every meal she'd concocted from the sparsest of ingredients, every small luxury she'd done without—had been for love of him. And, of course, for the hope of a brighter future; he was right about that. But no amount of money could possibly compensate for those blasted hopes. Any kind of payment would simply reduce their marriage to a cash bargain, and it would reduce Paige to the status of a paid employee instead of a once-treasured wife...

And perhaps that was the way he'd always looked at it, she told herself dispassionately. Eileen certainly thought that Austin had never intended to stay with her, once the advantages of marriage had faded and once he was firmly established on his own path to success.

If that was the case, Paige thought, she'd just as soon not have it confirmed.

"You don't need to buy me off," she said.

"That's not what I'm doing. If I'd had anything at the time of the divorce, you'd have gotten your share."

Paige shrugged. "That was the gamble I took. I put my money in the slot machine and there wasn't any payoff. It wouldn't be fair to complain just because the next person who dropped in a quarter hit the jackpot."

"In other words," he said evenly, "marrying me turned up lemons."

"Too green and sour even to make lemonade with," Paige said. "If that stings, Austin—well, maybe it's just because the truth often does. In any case, if I took your money it probably wouldn't make you feel better and it would darn sure not make me happy. So why don't we just drop—"

The sonorous notes of the doorbell cut her off.

Austin glanced at his watch with a puzzled look and strode across the hall to answer it.

Beyond the half-open door, Paige could see only a

gleam of red fabric, but she had no trouble identifying the voice. Feminine, sultry, suggestive…but what was the building super doing at a tenant's apartment at midnight?

"I don't know what I was thinking, Austin," Tricia Cade gushed. "I had such a good time at your party tonight that I forgot all about you having to take a babysitter home."

Paige was startled. Austin had taken Tricia Cade to Sabrina's dinner party? But he'd seemed so anxious to get rid of her the day he'd moved in…

Or perhaps he hadn't been turned off by Tricia that day, he just hadn't wanted any witnesses to his first confrontation with Paige. And though Paige hadn't thought the super was quite Austin's type… Well, after all these years, how would she know what kind of woman interested him? Even when she'd been married to the man she obviously hadn't known him as well as she'd thought she had, or she'd have suspected the existence of Marliss Howard. So how could she possibly predict his tastes now?

"I'll be happy to stay with Jennifer while you—" Tricia had stepped far enough into the hallway to see Paige, and she stopped dead.

"No need," Paige said placidly. "I have my own transportation." She tucked her screwdriver back into her tote bag and took her coat from the back of a chair in the living room. "Austin, please tell Jennifer I had a lovely evening."

He followed her into the hallway. "I don't much like the idea of you driving across town at this hour."

"You should have thought of that earlier," Paige pointed out. "Anyway, I do it all the time."

"I'd appreciate a call to let me know you're home safe."

"Tricia wouldn't appreciate it," Paige murmured. "And

in any case, it's not your place to be worried about me anymore, Austin. That's all been over for years.''

She walked away, her footsteps hushed in the carpeted corridor. And as she got into the elevator, she couldn't help but see that he was still standing just outside his apartment, one hand on the half-open door.

Paige dreamed that Austin came into her bedroom in the middle of the night.

It was clearly the bedroom in her bungalow, with its ruffled white curtains and brass bed, and not the room they'd shared in the cheap student-housing development— so she knew, even while it was happening, that it could only be a dream. Still, in her mind she reacted exactly as she had so many times during their brief marriage—with arms upraised to welcome him, her body already tingling with desire before he'd even touched her...

She woke with a jolt. Her mouth was dry, her breasts ached, and her breath came in painful gasps, as if she really had been making love.

No doubt, she told herself, the whole sequence had been inspired because spending the night with him had been so clearly what Tricia Cade had in mind. Paige wondered if the woman had succeeded.

You don't care, she told herself. *You simply do not care.*

She reached for a magazine and turned pages without seeing what was on them until it was time to get up.

The coffeemaker was just finishing its cycle when Eileen wheeled her chair in from her bedroom at the back of the first floor. ''You were very late last night. What were you doing?'' she asked.

''Precisely what I told you, Mother. I was looking after a little girl for a client.'' It might not be the entire truth, Paige thought, but if Eileen didn't know the details—like the fact that the client was Austin—she couldn't make a fuss about them.

"I tried to call you. There was no answer."

"On my cell phone? That's impossible." Paige reached for the tote bag she'd dropped on a kitchen chair when she'd come in last night. Her phone was still in the side pocket, but when she pulled it out the display was blank. "Jen—" She stopped herself. She remembered Jennifer turning the phone on, after its fall. But the child must have switched it off again before putting it back in the bag. "I'm sorry," she said. "It was an accident, Mother, and I'll make sure it doesn't get shut off again. What happened?"

"I'm just glad I wasn't having a health crisis."

Paige felt a little chilly at the possibility herself. "That's what emergency services are for," she said, as much to herself as to Eileen.

Eileen sniffed. "I tried to reach you because that Ben Orcutt called again."

Paige wanted to groan. "About his dishes? I don't know when I'll get to him. It'll have to be tomorrow, I suppose, or he'll be reduced to eating out of a can with his fingers."

"Has the man never heard of disposable plates?"

"It's not that, Mother. I told you he's lonely."

"Right. If he calls again, I'm going to tell him to let the dishes keep piling up and just put out a welcome sign for the cockroaches. Then he'll have all the company he can handle. Did you bring the newspaper in?"

"I'll get it."

By the time Paige came back from the front step with the bulky Sunday paper, Eileen had poured a cup of coffee and wheeled herself over to the table, and the telephone was ringing.

Sabrina, sounding bright and cheerful, said, "I'm glad

to catch you, Paige. I tried your cell phone last night after the party."

"It was turned off," Paige admitted.

"I gathered that. You'll notice I'm not asking why—or because of whom. But just between us, darling, *good for you!*"

Paige dragged the phone into the next room, out of Eileen's earshot. "There was no man involved."

"Whatever you say, Paige. I have to warn you, though, next time, you're not getting off so easily. You should have seen the woman Austin brought to my party to fill the empty space you left."

"I have seen her."

Sabrina was silent for a moment. "Oh, that's right— she's the super at Aspen Towers, isn't she? Why didn't you warn me that he was bringing a vamp?"

"Because he didn't check out the idea with me before he invited her," Paige said dryly.

"That's a thought," Sabrina murmured. "Shall I suggest to him that next time he ask your advice?"

Paige knew very well that it had been only a matter of days since either Cassie or Sabrina had dealt with Ben Orcutt's dirty dishes, but the mess she faced on Monday morning was the most daunting she'd ever seen in his kitchen. "Looks like you've been having parties, Ben," she said as she filled the sink with suds and dug her favorite rubber gloves out of her tote bag.

"No, it's just me. I'm sorry to be such a nuisance, you know, but—"

"You're not a nuisance, Ben. I wondered, though, have you ever thought of inviting some of your neighbors over? Maybe they'd like to play cards in the evening or something."

"But that would just make more dishes for you."

Paige thought she saw his eyes brighten at the idea; more dishes meant more frequent visits from Rent-A-Wife... "You can serve snacks and chips straight from the bag," she recommended.

She had just plunged the first stack of plates into the steaming water when her cell phone rang. She swore under her breath, dried off her hands, and slipped one hand out of her rubber glove so she could manipulate the phone's buttons.

"Is this Paige?" The little voice was almost trembling.

"Jennifer? What's wrong?"

"The school can't find my daddy."

Whatever that meant, Paige thought. "How'd you manage to call me?"

"When I turned your phone on the other night, I saw the number light up."

"And remembered it?" The kid was a midget accountant, Paige thought. "What's up?"

"It's cold. I can see my breath."

"Yes, it's cold. It's supposed to snow in a day or two. It's Denver, and it's December. But Jennifer, we've had this talk before, and I'm a little busy right now, so—"

"No, I mean it's cold *inside*." Jennifer sounded desperate. "The heat won't run."

"You mean the furnace is broken in the school?"

She could almost hear Jennifer's nod. "And they want us to go home right away. But I can't go anywhere, because the school can't find my daddy."

That figures, Paige thought. *Austin hasn't changed much—he's never there when he's needed.* "I'll come and get you right away, honey." She clicked the phone off, gave the antenna a shove, and said, "I'm really sorry, Ben, but I have to go deal with an emergency. I'll be back as soon as I can."

"I didn't know you had a little girl."

"I don't," Paige said. She stripped off her other rubber glove and dropped the pair beside the sink.

"Odd," Ben Orcutt murmured. "It certainly sounds as if you do."

CHAPTER FIVE

THE Larrimer Academy was only a few blocks from Aspen Towers, but the two buildings could not have been less alike, Paige thought as she hurried up the sidewalk to the school, holding the hood of her coat with both hands so the gusty wind wouldn't blow it off her head.

Aspen Towers was sleek and painfully modern, all steel and glass, while the academy was housed in a Victorian mansion left over from the days when silver had been king in Colorado. Paige supposed it should have been no surprise that the heating system had broken down; it could well be as old as the house. Why replace something that worked quite adequately, she could almost hear the head of the school saying, when the money could be better used for new textbooks and improved equipment?

She found Jennifer in a classroom which had once been the house's front parlor, part of a small group of students who were bundled in their winter coats against the distinctly chilly atmosphere. The moment she stepped into the room, Jennifer threw down a crayon and ran to meet her.

The teacher in charge looked alarmed for a moment, until she recognized Paige.

"I'm taking Jennifer to her father's office," Paige announced, and the teacher nodded, obviously relieved to have one more of her students safely settled.

When Jennifer had buckled herself into the back seat of Paige's minivan, she held out her hands to the stream of warm air coming from the vents. "I hate it here," she announced. "I want to go home."

"To Atlanta, you mean? You can take that question up with your father, as soon as we find him." Paige calculated the fastest route and made a U-turn to get onto the most direct street.

At Tanner Electronics, she marched a reluctant Jennifer through the atrium and up to the executive wing. "Why do I have to go to daddy's office?" the child asked mulishly.

"Because there's no one to look after you at the apartment."

Jennifer blinked in obvious surprise. "There's you."

From a five-year-old's point of view, Paige thought, it was an eminently sensible statement.

Outside the closed door of the office which had been Caleb's, sitting at the secretary's desk, was a stiffly-starched middle aged woman who looked from Paige to Jennifer with distaste. Her presence alone was enough to tell Paige that the planned office switch had taken place; not only had Caleb Tanner never bothered with a secretary, but the playboy entrepreneur would have slit his throat with a silicon wafer before hiring one who was less than pleasant to the eye.

"I'm looking for Austin Weaver," Paige said briskly. "His daughter needs him."

"Are you from the school? I gave him the message as soon as I could, and I'm sure he'll handle it when he has time. There was no need to take matters into your own hands."

Paige said grimly, "There was every need. Where is he?"

"Mr. Weaver is not available." The secretary's voice was prim.

"Then we'll wait until he's available again. Unless you'd like to look after Jennifer in the meantime?"

Just as Paige had expected, the secretary shrank back in her chair and waved a hand toward the inner office. "He's out of the building," she said. "But I suppose you can wait in there."

Paige had expected the office to look bare, but she was startled. For the first time ever, she could see the top of the desk, for it was no longer the electronic junk bin it had resembled in Caleb's day. However, piled along one end and reaching more than a foot high were folders and papers, books and computer disks.

It looked, she thought, as if Austin had his work cut out for him. He didn't need an In basket, he needed an annex.

The first hour of their wait passed in relative peace. At the end of it, however, Jennifer flounced in her chair and complained, "If we went to the apartment, we could at least read stories."

Paige looked around in desperation. "Here's a pencil and the Wall Street Journal. Circle all the words you recognize. It'll be good practice."

Jennifer rolled her eyes but she took the pencil and paper.

No more than five minutes later Austin burst through the door. "Paige? What in the hell do you think you're doing?"

Jennifer observed, without looking up from the newspaper, "That's a naughty word, Daddy."

"Warm greetings to you, too," Paige said. "I could ask where the…where you've been, but now that you're here, I really don't care."

"I've been at the school. I got there as soon as I could, only to find that Jennifer was missing. When I finally found a teacher who could tell me whom she'd left with, I still didn't have any hint where you'd gone. I tried the apartment—"

"Why?" Paige interrupted.

"Because you still have a key."

"Oh. I forgot to give it to you, after all, didn't I?"

"So I finally came back here so I could start organizing some kind of search, and the minute I walk in my secretary greets me with the news that you're in my office."

"It seemed the logical place to find you in the middle of a workday. Speaking of your new secretary—"

"I know," Austin said shortly. "She doesn't have particularly good judgment, which is why she didn't pass on the school's message to me right away. She's a temp, okay? Just till I have a chance to interview, which—at this rate—looks as if it will be never. This is not a good time to be running around dealing with details. My first day on the job—"

"Don't threaten to bite me," Paige said. "I've heard it all before, so there's no point in wasting more time trying to convince me how important your business is. Your daughter is not a detail."

Austin was obviously taken aback. "I didn't say she was, Paige. I said I had better things to do than chase you all over town."

"Well, the chasing's done with, so you can relax now. Have a good time together." Paige turned on her heel.

A much different note in his voice stopped her at the door. "Paige—"

She didn't turn around.

Austin came across the room. "Thanks for taking care of her. I'm sorry for yelling at you. I was scared, when I couldn't find her."

"Yeah." Paige's voice was gruff. "I can understand that."

"But I shouldn't have taken it out on you. Look, can I buy you lunch somewhere?" Austin asked.

"I'm hungry, Daddy," Jennifer said.

Paige raised an eyebrow at him.

"I mean both of you, of course."

She shook her head. "Thanks, but I've got a load of work to do. It was already a heavy day before I lost a couple of hours. And before you offer to pay me for my time, don't bother. I'll just put it on the company's bill as services provided to executive staff."

He didn't protest, which surprised Paige. "You're determined to be independent, aren't you? You didn't call me when you got home the other night, either."

"I told you I wouldn't, Austin."

"What harm would it have done to check in? I'd have called you, but I didn't have your number."

"Ask Jennifer next time," Paige said with a tinge of humor. "She seems to have my cell phone down pat."

"And the regular number?"

"Persistent, aren't you? It's in the book, under Rent-A-Wife."

"Your home is also Rent-A-Wife?"

"Is there something wrong with home-based businesses, oh great executive?"

"No. But something's wrong with your life if you don't need a separate number for your friends."

"Thanks for that insight," Paige said gently. "I'll remember to call you next time I need counseling." She retraced her steps and held out a hand to Jennifer. "See you later, kid."

Jennifer pushed her hand aside and gave her a hug instead.

Paige, startled by the sudden gesture, happened to look over the child's shoulder at Austin. His eyes were narrowed, his face thoughtful, and there were two tiny furrows between his brows.

He looked, she speculated, as if he'd seen something he didn't much like.

Well, that was no surprise. The only real question was why it should make her feel sad.

Austin didn't take Jennifer out for lunch, after all; he sent his secretary for take-out. And a good decision that had been, Austin thought as he watched his daughter stack cold French fries into a sort of split-rail fence along the edge of his desk. His own sandwich had long since been disposed of and he'd returned to work, but his gaze kept straying from the spreadsheets in front of him to the child's ketchup-smeared face.

There was no doubt that Jennifer preferred chicken nuggets and fries out of a paper bag to more sophisticated fare and more elegant surroundings. He couldn't quite say the same for himself. In fact, he wished he'd asked the secretary to bring him some antacid for dessert.

Still, it was just as well that Paige hadn't taken him up on his offer to buy her lunch. His invitation had been so impulsive he'd been surprised himself when the words popped out, and she'd looked just as startled as he'd felt.

She'd looked, in fact, as if she wanted to ask what on earth they would find to talk about. The old days, maybe? The days when any restaurant with a tablecloth was above their budget—so far out of reach, in fact, that some weeks a walk to the neighborhood shop for a soft-serve ice cream cone was the height of extravagance. Who wanted to be reminded of things like that?

Though in fact, he thought, there had been something almost magical about the evenings when they'd walked home in the twilight, and he'd watched as her tongue darted over the cold confection, and he'd ended up hungry for a lot more than ice cream....

"Daddy?" Jennifer sounded impatient. "I told you, I'm done."

"Then tear down the French fry fence and put it in the wastebasket," he said absently.

Nostalgia was all very well, he thought, if it involved events and situations which were safely in the past. Which was true of their marriage, of course—for both of them, it was long over and done with. But where money was concerned...

He could afford to be nostalgic about twilight walks and ice cream cones. But he had the feeling, despite Paige's protestations that her business was doing very well indeed, that financially she hadn't come so very far from the soft-ice-cream days.

And he found himself starting to wonder if they couldn't work out some kind of a deal.

The first thing Paige saw when she stepped into the bungalow's kitchen that evening was the single pink rose in a white china vase and surrounded by asparagus fern and baby's breath, which sat in the middle of the table.

The first thing she heard was her mother's voice, coming from the living room. "There's water in the sink, you said? Good for you, getting that far by yourself."

The sarcasm in Eileen's tone was thick enough to slice, Paige thought, and felt a rush of sympathy for whoever was on the receiving end of it.

She reached for the tiny card which was tucked in among the baby's breath and realized the envelope had already been opened. *Now I'm in for it,* she thought.

Eileen wheeled her chair around the corner into the kitchen, cupped her hand over the telephone and stared at Paige. "Who's Jennifer," she asked, "and why is she sending you flowers?"

The tightness in Paige's chest relaxed a bit, and she looked at the card. *Thank you from Jennifer* was all it said. She didn't think for a moment that the rose had actually been Jennifer's idea, but at least Austin hadn't caused unnecessary problems by signing his own name. "Since when do you open my cards?" she countered.

"The only thing on the envelope was the address," Eileen said. "I was trying to make sure it was correct. So who's Jennifer?"

"The little girl I was taking care of Saturday night."

"Is this a policy change? If Rent-A-Wife's taking payment in roses now, I think I should know about it."

"It wouldn't be the first time a grateful client has done more to show appreciation than simply write a check."

Eileen looked sharply at her, but just then Paige heard a murmur from the other end of the telephone that commanded her mother's attention once more.

"No," Eileen said firmly, "if the water's been in the sink since this morning, you can't use it." She wheeled herself over to the stove and lifted the lid on a pan. "I don't care if it's still clean, it'll be cold. Empty the sink and run some more. And make it hot enough to give off steam."

Paige touched a velvety pink petal, loosing a torrent of scent. "What are you doing, Mother?"

"Taking things into my own hands." Eileen's voice was tart. "And trying to cover up for you, I might add. Someone has to wash Ben Orcutt's dishes, and since you didn't show up and I can't go over there and do it myself—"

Paige closed her eyes in pain. "I can't believe I forgot Ben Orcutt's dishes." But in fact, she realized, it was a wonder she hadn't forgotten a whole lot more; her encounter with Austin had knocked any idea of orderliness from the rest of her day. Anything that hadn't been on her

carefully prepared list—and Ben Orcutt had been an extra—had gone completely out of her mind.

"I know you forgot," Eileen said. "He called to tell
me all about it. Is the water run yet, Mr. Orcutt? What did
you say? No, you may *not* bring the dirty dishes here.
Whatever you think it sounded like, I was not volunteering
to do your housework. Do you have a pair of rubber
gloves?"

"Tell him I'll come this evening," Paige said. "In fact,
I'll come right now."

Eileen covered the phone again. "Don't be ridiculous.
He'd be perfectly capable if you just hadn't pampered him
by letting him depend on you."

"You've never met Ben Orcutt," Paige warned. But
Eileen had plunged into step-by-step instructions, and there
was obviously no point in trying to interrupt the flow.

I'll stop by tomorrow morning, Paige thought, *and clear
up the mess.* She just hoped that between them, Ben and
Eileen didn't flood his kitchen in the meantime.

She changed into jeans and a sweatshirt and was just
coming down the stairs, intending to tackle Rent-A-Wife's
accounts receivable, when the doorbell rang. Eileen, she
noted, had only begun the rinse stage, so Paige peeked out
through the viewer and swore at what she saw.

She pulled the door open a couple of inches and said,
"Do you have a suicide wish? What if my mother had
answered the door?"

Austin shrugged. "The dragon on wheels would have
either slammed it in my face or given me a piece of her
mind. Or she might have done the totally unexpected and
been pleasant, which would have come closer to giving me
a heart attack. Besides, Jennifer saw your van and knew
you were home, so I figured we had a fifty-fifty chance."

Jennifer accused, "You didn't tell me you had a kid, Paige."

Paige shook her head, confused. "I don't. What makes you think—" She followed the child's pointing finger. "Oh, the second peek hole in the door?"

Jennifer nodded. "It's just my size." She demonstrated.

"Well, it's also just the right size for my mother. When she's sitting in her wheelchair, she can't see out the top one, so we added an extra."

Jennifer looked disappointed.

"What can I do for you, Austin?"

"Come for a walk. Just around the block."

From the kitchen, Paige heard her mother say, "Now just keep doing that, one plate at a time, and before you know it you'll be done."

It was apparent that the conversation would be finished any minute now, and then Eileen would no doubt wheel into the living room to see who had rung the bell. Paige reached for a heavy jacket and called, "I'm going out for a few minutes, Mother." Before Eileen could have a chance to respond, Paige was on the doorstep, closing the door behind her.

"But I don't want to go for a walk," Jennifer grumbled. "I'm cold!"

"If you don't stop saying that," Austin warned, "your vocal cords will lock into position and you won't be able to say anything else."

"Really?" Jennifer sounded half doubtful, but she brightened immediately. "Hey, then I wouldn't have to answer any of the teachers' questions at school. I'm cold. I'm cold. I'm—"

Paige had to bite her lip to keep from giggling.

Austin sighed. "That was not quite the result I had in mind." He started down the sidewalk.

Paige dug her hands into her pockets. Automatically, her stride lengthened as she dropped into step beside him and picked up the half-remembered rhythm of walking together. She soon realized what she was doing, and this time, when she bit her lip, it wasn't to control her sense of humor.

The last time she'd gone for a walk with him, she remembered, was before he'd told her he was leaving Denver. When she had still thought everything was wonderful and that their love would shine forever....

Jennifer trailed behind them, hopping over sidewalk cracks and muttering to herself. Paige glanced over her shoulder to be sure the child wasn't listening. "To tell the truth," she said, "I'm a little cold myself. So what do you want, Austin?"

"I've got a problem."

"And here I thought you were just nostalgic for a cheap date," Paige mocked. Too late, she regretted reminding him of the many hours they'd spent on walks during their brief marriage. He might suspect that she dwelled on her memories of their shared and inexpensive entertainments, while in fact, she told herself firmly, she did nothing of the kind.

But Austin didn't seem to notice. "The latest report from the academy is that there will be no school tomorrow, and probably not for the next few days."

Paige gave a soft whistle. "The furnace blew up that badly, hmm?"

"Apparently it's a vintage model, and getting parts could take a while."

"I hope Jennifer liked your office. You might want to take some books tomorrow, though."

"Not a bad idea. I understand I have you to thank for the fact that in my copy of Tanner's latest budget and annual report to stockholders, all the easy-to-read words are circled.''

Paige winced. "I didn't give her the stockholders' report, only the newspaper.''

"Once started, she showed no discretion.''

"Sorry about that.''

Austin shrugged. "The point is, I can't make her sit in my office all week while I work, Paige. It would be cruel to her.''

"To say nothing of being dangerous to your office,'' she murmured. "Welcome to the joys of single parenthood.''

"And I can't take time off after one day on the job—especially this job. I'm up to my neck in complications here.''

"Things aren't running as smoothly at Tanner as you thought they were going to?''

Austin shot a look at her. "Not exactly,'' he admitted. "Stuff that should have been handled weeks ago was simply left to wait for the new CEO, and the minute I walked in, it all descended on me.''

Paige shrugged. "I guess in that case you'd better call the nanny and tell her that vacation time is over. Rent-A-Wife will meet her plane, if you like—we go back and forth to the airport at least a couple of times a week on errands like that.''

"She's not coming to Denver at all.''

"Why? Didn't she like the climate any more than Jennifer does? Then I suppose you'll have to hire another one.''

"By tomorrow? You have no idea how hard it is to find someone who's qualified.''

"No,'' Paige said judiciously. "I haven't had that problem. In the meantime, I'm sure Tricia Cade would help you out. The way she so enthusiastically volunteered Saturday night... After Jennifer was safely asleep, of course, but I'm sure that was only coincidence."

"And Jennifer really would like that idea, too," Austin said dryly. "She'd be marching a picket line by the end of the first day. Unless she drew circles on a rental contract and Tricia hung her from the top of the building."

Paige couldn't stop herself. "Does Jennifer even know you took Tricia to a party?"

Austin didn't answer. "I really thought we could make this work," he said heavily. "With Jennifer in school every day, in an academy that offers all sorts of after-school activities, I thought we could surely get along without a nanny."

"Sounds like wishful thinking to me." With relief, Paige noted that they'd turned the final corner and her house was just a few yards away.

"But this is the kind of thing Rent-A-Wife does all the time, right?"

"No, it's not," Paige said hastily. "We do not baby-sit."

"What about Saturday night?"

"That was a special arrangement. A favor for my partner, not for you. There's a lot of difference between transporting a kid from school to soccer practice and taking care of one all day. I have a job, too, Austin. In fact, I have a lot of jobs."

"But you can't deny that your day is a lot more flexible than mine is right now."

"And that's exactly why you need a long-term solution."

"I'm working on it, all right?" Austin sounded frustrated. "I'm just trying to buy a little time so I can figure something out."

Jennifer's small hand stole into Paige's. "There's a kitty up there under the bushes," she confided.

"Besides," Austin said, "she likes you."

Paige surveyed the shadows under the spreading juniper bushes in front of her bungalow, but what she was really seeing was the stacks of paper on Austin's desk and the prim and frosty secretary just outside his door—and the face of the child who stood by her side, her to-the-bone chill forgotten for the moment simply because she had caught a glimpse of a stray cat.

Paige sighed. "I'll see you in the morning. At the apartment? Or shall I pick her up at the office?"

Austin smiled. There was relief in his face, and gratitude, and something more, as well—something that hit Paige with the force of a thousand volts.

She hadn't forgotten how devastatingly effective his charm could be, but she'd convinced herself she was long past succumbing to its effects. He'd lost that power over her the day he'd told her he was leaving.

Or at least that was what she had believed.

Now, however, Paige was dizzy and almost breathless. As if, she thought, she'd put one foot down on a very slippery slope, and she could feel herself starting to slide.

Only it was too late to back away.

The atrium lobby at Tanner Electronics looked different. The lights overhead seemed brighter somehow, almost glaring against the glass panels. At first Paige thought the change was simply because she'd never been there so early in the morning, before the weak winter sun gained enough altitude to produce adequate light to compete with the artificial glow.

Then she saw the ropes blocking off a good third of the atrium, channeling traffic from the front doors to a big new circular desk which stood precisely in the center of the lobby. As she paused to stare, a uniformed security guard came up to her. "Excuse me, miss. I'll need you to sign in at the desk and show some identification. Are you an employee or a visitor?"

Stunned, Paige complied. Finally, with a brand-new neon-green visitor's badge clipped to the breast pocket of her navy camel hair blazer, she made it to the executive wing.

Austin was already at his desk, and Jennifer was sprawled on her stomach on the carpet with a book open in front of her, waving her sneakered feet in the air, when Paige came in.

"It took you a long time," Jennifer accused.

"Don't push your luck, Jen," Austin recommended. He tossed down his fountain pen and stood.

"It's not my fault if I'm late," Paige said. "Blame the idiot who insists everybody in the building have a new fashion accessory." She flicked a finger against the badge.

"What's so bad about them?"

"How would you know? I don't see you wearing one." Paige's eyes narrowed. "This was your idea, wasn't it?"

Silently, Austin picked up his sports jacket from the back of a chair and displayed his badge.

"At least yours looks decent," Paige grumbled. "I bet mine will glow in the dark."

"Point taken. Maybe we can find a different color that will still make visitors stand out without being quite so loud."

"Oh, that's a minor detail. As long as you're noting objections, how about this one? Do you have any idea how many times I come into this building in the average week? If I have to stand in line to be approved every time—"

"Once the security people start recognizing faces, things

will move a lot faster. And maybe we can create a sort of permanent visitors' identification system to speed things up.''

''I am humbly grateful. Come on, Jennifer, let's get out of here so your daddy can get to work.'' She helped the child gather up her backpack. It wasn't particularly heavy, she noted, but it was stuffed so full that the zipper was straining. Jennifer must have brought along all her favorite things. ''And so I can turn this badge in and stop feeling like a billboard,'' she added, with a sideways look at Austin.

Jennifer skipped down the hall beside her, swinging the backpack. ''What are we going to do today?''

''Nothing too exciting, I'm afraid. Dishes, for one thing. Drop off a bag of laundry at the dry cleaner's. Stop at the newspaper office to buy a back issue. Pick up a fur coat at the storage place and take it to the owner's house....''

Jennifer's eyes, she noted, were starting to glaze. Paige laughed. ''At least it will be more fun than sitting in your dad's office drawing circles. You can help me plan a Christmas party, too.''

''I like parties,'' Jennifer said. ''Once I went to a birthday party, and—''

Her chatter kept up as they walked all the way through the building to the balcony above the atrium, where Paige stopped dead. What about her plans to hold a Christmas banquet for Tanner's entire work force in that lobby? A brand-new and enormous security station carved out of the exact center of the room was hardly the kind of focal point she'd had in mind.

''Back to the drawing board,'' she muttered, and retreated to the cafeteria to commandeer a booth so she could start revising plans.

She was still at it an hour later when Sabrina, wearing

a neon-green badge that matched Paige's, came in for a cup of coffee. "What are you doing here?" Sabrina asked. "Isn't it my day to satisfy the whims of Tanner employees? Not that the job couldn't keep two of us busy." She stirred sweetener into her coffee. "Hi, babe, why aren't you in school?"

"I'm not a babe," said the child with dignity.

"Long story," Paige muttered.

"You mean she's with you? I figured she'd just slipped away from her father to pick up some of the cafeteria's exquisite cuisine."

Paige made a point of shuffling through her papers.

"Don't want to talk about it?" Sabrina asked. "Okay. Guess what my mother's done this time."

"I don't think I want to know," Paige said honestly.

"I've started getting response cards from people I didn't invite to the wedding, telling me how pleased they are to be able to come."

"She's been calling them up?"

"Oh, nothing so crass. She had an extra set of invitations engraved, and she's been helpfully sending them to people I had, according to her, overlooked."

"Will they all fit in the church?"

"Are you kidding? I was having trouble enough before she started. Besides, don't you think that's beside the point, Paige?"

"Maybe. But she is your mother, after all."

"And she's being abominable."

"That's just part of her nature, Sabrina. As trying as it is, if you want to have your mother be a part of your life—"

"I know, I know. I'm just not sure, sometimes, that I do. My entire existence was a lot more peaceful when my parents were still disowning me." Her face brightened. "I know what will make me feel better. Caleb's going out of town for a couple of days. He says it's business, but—''

"I don't blame him for leaving," Paige said. "He probably wants to get out of range till the employees adjust to the shock of the new security system. I just hope he's not counting on them getting over it anytime soon."

"Actually, I think he's grabbing at any chance that comes along to avoid my mother until the wedding. Anyway, he's leaving at noon, so let's have a slumber party tonight at my condo. It'll be the last chance before my wedding for you and Cassie and me to eat junk food and act like teenagers and—''

Jennifer said, "I want to come to the party."

"You'll be home with your daddy," Paige said.

"Actually," Sabrina mused, "she won't. That's why I thought of the idea in the first place—because Caleb's taking Jake and Austin with him, so Cassie will be at loose ends with her husband gone. And Jennifer... I wonder what Austin does plan to do with Jennifer." She looked at Paige with a frown. "Honey?"

So that's why Jennifer's backpack looked as if she'd stuffed her entire wardrobe into it, Paige thought. Because she had.

"Honey?" Sabrina repeated. "Why are you suddenly staring at me as if your face is frozen?"

CHAPTER SIX

AUSTIN knew from the instant that Paige burst into his office that he was as good as dead. In fact, he knew it even before that, the moment he heard her talking to his secretary on the other side of the closed door.

He raised his voice a little to try to drown her out. "The main objectives of the trip, gentlemen—"

Tanner's other two top executives exchanged a glance. "Sounds like one of your ex-girlfriends out there, Caleb," Jake Abbott murmured. "Haven't you got rid of the bimbo contingent yet?"

"They're not all that easy to get rid of," Caleb said. "But my guess is that's no bimbo. In fact, if I didn't know better, I'd say it sounds like—"

The office door burst open; Paige stood on the threshold and glared. "Dammit, Austin!"

"—Paige," Caleb finished casually. "What a pleasure." But the surprise in his face, Austin thought, belied his airy tone.

Austin stole a look at Jake, who was rubbing his chin and looking at the carpet as if he couldn't decide whether to be amused or dismayed.

Obviously, Austin thought, neither of them was used to seeing Paige in full fury. *What a distinction it is,* he told himself wryly, *to be the only one to bring out that side of her.*

"I gather you got my message," Austin said.

Paige dug her fists into her hips. "If you mean, has the

grapevine got to me yet with the word that you're leaving town, yes!''

"You know," Jake murmured, "this scene has some familiar overtones. I seem to remember Cassie having the same sort of—"

The interruption seemed to steady her. Paige shot a look at Jake and made an obvious effort to pull herself together. "I'm sorry to intrude on your discussion," she said, sounding nothing of the sort. "But when I heard the news about this business trip, I was naturally somewhat concerned about—"

Caleb nodded wisely. "She was somewhat concerned," he told Jake.

"Of course she was," Jake agreed.

Austin saw the gathering fire in Paige's eyes and hastily intervened. "Thanks for trying to help, guys, but if you wouldn't mind…"

"Mind getting out while we still can?" Caleb asked. "Not at all. Believe me." He was already on his feet as he spoke.

The door closed behind the two of them, and silence descended on the office. Austin gestured invitingly toward the chairs that Jake and Caleb had occupied. Paige ignored the suggestion and continued to stand in the middle of the office, eyes narrowed, watching him.

Finally she said quietly, "It occurs to me all of a sudden that I may have just made a complete fool of myself. I stormed in here assuming that you intend to dump your responsibilities on me. But if you've already arranged for Jennifer's care while you're gone, I owe you an apology."

Apart from the nasty crack about responsibilities, he thought, she sounded calm—almost friendly. *Too bad that can't last.*

He leaned on his desk for a little extra support as he bit

the bullet. "Actually, no, I hadn't finalized any plans for Jennifer. I was hoping that you—"

"You were *hoping?*" Paige's voice had started to rise again. "Let me tell you, Austin, you have an incredible nerve! Expecting me to be on call for you, without even *asking*—"

"I didn't assume anything," Austin said hastily. "I tried to ask, Paige. I left a message for you to call me. And I'm really sorry you heard about this from someone else first."

"I'll just bet you are." Her voice dripped sarcasm. "You left a message for me? Why? I was right here in the building, dammit!"

"How should I know that?" he asked, trying to keep his tone reasonable.

"Your precious security gangsters could have told you. Isn't that the whole point, that they know where every warm body is at any given moment? I figured they'd hooked the badges to a satellite locator!"

"You said you were anxious to get rid of the badge, so I assumed you'd already gone. I didn't even call downstairs to ask."

She frowned a little. "Then where did you leave a message?"

"With your mother."

"You told my mother that you want me to look after your kid while you go out of town? I'll bet that left her speechless."

"I didn't give her the details. I just asked for you to call. I suppose she sabotaged me by losing the message."

"She knows better than to do that. But it's no wonder she didn't pass it on right away—she's not likely to think I was dying to hear from you. So what are the details?"

The level tone of her voice didn't deceive him. He wasn't out of the woods yet.

He moved around the end of his desk and perched on the corner. "The trip came up very suddenly. Just this morning, in fact. We were discussing the problems Tanner's facing—"

"It seems a bit odd," Paige mused, "if it's such a new idea, that Sabrina already knows all about it."

"Not really. She happened to pop her head in a few minutes ago, just as Caleb suggested that we make a fast tour of Tanner's facilities and visit a couple of major clients."

"And when the boss suggests something, you jump."

"In this case," Austin said coolly, "I'm the boss. That doesn't mean I don't listen to advice. Under these circumstances, I think it's a wise move, because going right now may prevent months of problems down the line."

"Don't waste your breath trying to convince me. I already know that once you've made up your mind, it would take two archangels and a heavenly chorus to change it."

Austin decided, wrong though she was, that it would be prudent not to argue the point just now. "I'll be gone a couple of days, three at the top end."

"And you need someone to look after Jennifer," she mused.

"I'd expect to pay for the services, of course."

"Is money always the first thing you think of, Austin? What if I say no?"

He took a deep breath, and let it out very slowly. "I don't know what I'll do," he admitted.

The silence stretched out. She moved, finally, but only to walk across the room to the window and stand staring out toward the distant blue haze of the Rocky Mountains. "Just out of curiosity, Austin, back when you were deciding to dispense with a nanny, how did you plan to handle this kind of thing? Or didn't you anticipate ever having to leave town again?''

"You know," Austin said, "your mother's style of sarcasm doesn't fit very well on you." He watched with satisfaction as her face flushed pink. "The academy's got a boarding program, so when I enrolled Jennifer I arranged for her to stay there anytime I had to travel. But I didn't anticipate the heat going off at the school."

Paige nodded. "They're probably scrambling to find warm beds for the boarders they've already got, not taking on more. Well, I'm glad to have that clear. It makes me feel a little better to know that you're merely unlucky, not terminally irresponsible."

It was now or never, he thought. He slid off the edge of his desk and quietly crossed the room to join her at the window. She didn't look at him, but he knew she was aware of his closeness because he saw her body tighten as if she was ready to defend herself. "Will you do it, Paige? You're the only person Jennifer really knows in this whole city. The only one she doesn't see as a stranger."

He saw her shoulders sag for a moment, as if she was taking on the weight of the world, and he knew he'd won. Then she turned to face him, and he realized that *won* wasn't the right word at all.

"I'm not interested in your money," she said.

"I can afford to pay you, Paige. And I know your time is valuable."

"Besides, if you write a check, then you wouldn't owe me any favors—isn't that what you mean? Anyway, I didn't say you wouldn't have to pay, Austin. I just don't want cash."

Warily, he said, "Then what do you have in mind?"

She hesitated and looked out the window once more. "I want you to make peace with my mother."

How on earth did she expect him to pacify Eileen? The dragon on wheels hadn't had a good word—or even a neutral one—to say about him since the day he'd met her. Austin said slowly, "If you mean you want me to go groveling to tell her I was wrong—"

"I want you to do whatever it takes." She smiled almost grimly. "Oh, don't worry—I don't expect you to end up as best friends. And you don't need to fret about my ulterior motives, either, because I don't have any."

He hadn't even gotten that far. "I guess I just don't see why it matters."

"Don't you? Just a few minutes ago, you assumed that I hadn't gotten your message because Mother had suppressed it. Sabotage was the first thing that came to your mind."

"For good reason," Austin said dryly.

"I admit she's capable. She probably wouldn't lose the message altogether, but she might conveniently let it slip her mind for a while. That's what I'm talking about. If you're going to be in Denver, and if Rent-A-Wife continues to work with Tanner's employees, then from time to time there's going to be contact between the two of you. I'd just like not to be stuck in the middle of a war."

"So you want me to arrange a cease-fire," Austin said. "I can try, Paige, but I can't promise it'll happen overnight. And I can't speak for Eileen. She may want nothing to do with me."

"Then you'll just have to exercise your celebrated charm, won't you?" Paige didn't look at him, and her voice was as distant as the hazy blue Rockies. "Take it or leave it."

"I'll take it."

He thought for a moment she hadn't heard him, but finally she said, "Jennifer and I were in the cafeteria,

Here's a **HOT** offer for you!

Get set for a
sizzling summer read...

with **2 FREE ROMANCE BOOKS**
and a **FREE MYSTERY GIFT!**

NO CATCH! NO OBLIGATION TO BUY!

Simply complete and return this card and
you'll get **2 FREE BOOKS** and **A FREE GIFT**
– yours to keep!

Visit us online at
www.eHarlequin.com

- The first shipment is yours to keep, **absolutely free!**

- Enjoy the convenience of Harlequin Romance® books delivered
  right to your door, before they're available in stores!

- Take advantage of special low pricing for **Reader Service Members only!**

- After receiving your free books we hope you'll want to remain a
  subscriber. But the choice is always yours—to continue or cancel,
  any time at all! So why not take us up on this fabulous invitation,
  with no risk of any kind. You'll be glad you did!

316 HDL C26A

116 HDL C25Z
(H-R-OS-06/00)

Name:		
	(Please Print)	
Address:		Apt.#:
City:		
State/Prov.:		Zip/Postal Code:

▶ DETACH HERE AND MAIL CARD TODAY! ▼

The Harlequin Reader Service® —Here's how it works:

Accepting your 2 free books and gift places you under no obligation to buy anything. You may keep the books and gift and return the shipping statement marked "cancel." If you do not cancel, about a month later we'll send you 6 additional novels and bill you just $2.90 each in the U.S., or $3.34 each in Canada, plus 25¢ delivery per book and applicable taxes if any.* That's the complete price and — compared to cover prices of $3.50 each in the U.S. and $3.99 each in Canada — it's quite a bargain! You may cancel at any time, but if you choose to continue, every month we'll send you 6 more books, which you may either purchase at the discount price or return to us and cancel your subscription.

*Terms and prices subject to change without notice. Sales tax applicable in N.Y. Canadian residents will be charged applicable provincial taxes and GST.

If offer card is missing write to: Harlequin Reader Service, 3010 Walden Ave., P.O. Box 1867, Buffalo, NY 14240-1867

BUSINESS REPLY MAIL
FIRST-CLASS MAIL   PERMIT NO. 717   BUFFALO, NY

POSTAGE WILL BE PAID BY ADDRESSEE

HARLEQUIN READER SERVICE
3010 WALDEN AVE
PO BOX 1867
BUFFALO NY 14240-9952

NO POSTAGE
NECESSARY
IF MAILED
IN THE
UNITED STATES

working on plans for the Christmas party. Do you want me to bring her back up here to say goodbye?''

"I'll come down in a few minutes." He had to clear his throat. "And before you say it—I know you're doing this for Jennifer's sake, not for me. Thanks, Paige."

She turned to face him. Her usually hazel eyes had gone dark with pain, and at the sight his breath caught in his throat. He could feel the warmth of her; it was the closest they'd been, he thought, since the day their marriage had died.

He wondered if her skin was still as soft, and before he stopped to consider whether it was wise to pursue the question, he'd put out a hand to brush her cheek.

She pulled back abruptly, as if she found his touch revolting. But he knew it wasn't distaste he saw in her eyes, in the moment before she turned away. In fact, he was almost certain it was fear.

She walked out without another word, leaving the office door open behind her, and a moment later Caleb and Jake came back in.

"Congratulations," Caleb said cheerfully. "If you can survive that without losing any blood, you're practically immortal. Though I suppose you managed it by giving Paige everything she asked for?"

"Something like that," Austin said absently.

Fear, he thought. Yes, he was almost sure it had been fear. But was she afraid of him? Of herself? Of something else entirely?

Jake gave a low whistle. "Everything? I'd say that's a red flag, clear as day. Better watch yourself, pal."

Caleb nodded. "He's right. That's one dangerous woman."

They were both obviously dead serious, but Austin almost felt like laughing.

Paige, a dangerous woman...

As if, he thought, *I didn't already know that.*

When Paige got back to the cafeteria, Sabrina had appropriated a pair of scissors and was snipping paper napkins into intricate, delicate cut-out snowflakes while Jennifer watched, eyes wide.

"The child has never seen snow," Sabrina explained.

"Don't expect the real stuff to be exactly like Sabrina's examples." Paige frowned. "I thought it snowed sometimes in Atlanta. You've really never seen it?"

"I don't remember," Jennifer said. "Is my daddy already gone?"

Paige was faintly horrified at how matter-of-fact she sounded. Saying goodbye to her father—or rather, *not* saying goodbye—seemed to be a very common thing. "Not yet. He said he'd come down in a little while to see you before he goes. How would you like to stay with me till he gets home?"

"So much for my slumber party," Sabrina murmured.

Jennifer considered. "At your house? Can I see the kitty again?"

Paige had to search her memory before she remembered the cat Jennifer thought she'd spotted yesterday under the juniper bushes in front of the bungalow. "I doubt it. It's so cold outside today that the cat will probably have gone home where it's warm."

"You're taking her to your house?" Sabrina asked softly. "What's your mother going to say about that? She called, by the way, while you were gone. You forgot to take your cell phone with you."

"I'll call her in a minute."

"As soon as you figure out a likely story? *Mothers,*" Sabrina said. She made the word sound like an oath

"Eileen's got the tongue of a wasp, but at least she's generally up front about things. My mother, on the other hand, is about as straightforward as a snake—"

"She means well, Sabrina. And you only get married once. Don't ruin your wedding day by getting into a quarrel with your mother about things that aren't important."

Sabrina looked thoughtful. "You know, Paige, you may have a point there."

Behind her, Austin said, "Just let Mom have her way, in the name of keeping the peace. How long have you been practicing that philosophy with the dragon on wheels, Paige?"

"Already figuring out how to get out of the deal you made?" Paige asked gently.

"Of course not. But I don't have to like everything I do." He held out both arms to Jennifer, who tossed aside the paper snowflake she'd been unfolding and rushed to him.

"Dragon on wheels?" Sabrina was frowning. "Are you talking about Eileen?"

Hastily, Paige said, "As long as you're making changes around here, Austin, how about giving the industrial spies a breather while you bring the cafeteria up to the standard of a greasy spoon, at least?"

"Great idea," Sabrina chimed in. "I'm tired of bringing my lunch when I'm planning to be here all day. Which I am, more often than not. The more of Tanner's employees discover our services, the crazier it's getting around here. When, I ask you, am I supposed to do my regular work?"

"You pack your lunch?" Paige asked in astonishment. "Sabrina, you don't know the difference between a bread knife and an orange peeler."

Sabrina ignored her. "And last time, I could actually

have auctioned off my food to Tanner's hungry employees."

"Which says a great deal about the caliber of the vending machines," Paige muttered, "when you consider that Sabrina's idea of a sandwich is—"

"I'll get to it," Austin said. "But first things first." With a murmur into his daughter's ear and a final hug, he went out.

Looking just a little forlorn, Jennifer settled back into the booth with her half-unfolded snowflake.

Sabrina picked up the scissors again. "Paige, what deal were you talking to Austin about?"

Paige caught her breath involuntarily. "Keeping Jennifer," she said steadily. "What else? Now that I'm back, you don't have to entertain her any longer. Didn't you say you have plenty to do today?"

"And tomorrow, and the day after that," Sabrina agreed. "We really need to look for another partner. Too bad Jennifer's not just a little older. We could put her to work."

"She might like washing Ben Orcutt's dishes." Paige thought about confessing what had happened yesterday, but stopped herself. If Ben accepted her apology, there would be no need for Sabrina and Cassie to be upset by the details. And if he didn't, there would be plenty of time to share them.

Sabrina shook her head. "She can't take on that job—I don't think they make gas masks that small, and heaven knows you wouldn't dare expose a child to that mess without one." She asked carelessly, without looking at Paige, "Has he kissed you yet?"

"Who? Ben?"

"No, silly. Austin."

"Oh, *him*," Paige said. Deliberately, she kept her voice cool. "Only a few thousand times."

Sabrina laughed. "Better be careful who hears you say that, they might take you seriously. Anyway, watch out for him. You've heard the newest bit of gossip, haven't you? He's been on the job less than two days, and everybody in the building already knows that whatever Austin wants, Austin gets."

Paige watched Jennifer's small fingers patiently picking the snowflake apart. *Whatever Austin wants, Austin gets*— she didn't doubt that a bit. The evidence was right before her eyes.

Though she felt guilty about putting off the inevitable, Paige had deliberately left Ben Orcutt till the end of the workday. She had no idea what she was going to say to him. She'd built her business on a reputation for reliability, but this time she'd blown it—and she expected that he might find it difficult to forgive the fact that he had been the exception to her rule.

There simply was no adequate excuse for forgetting to come back to finish his job. To top that off, she'd probably have to apologize for her mother's tart treatment of him, as well; after all, the man had phoned with a legitimate complaint, and instead of satisfaction, or even an apology, he'd gotten a lecture on how to take care of himself....

She parked the minivan in the lot beside the towering apartment complex and leaned into the back to unbuckle Jennifer's seat belt. "Mr. Orcutt may be a little grumpy," she warned. "He's not angry with you, so whatever he says, you just ignore it. All right?"

Jennifer looked puzzled. "Is he mad at you?"

"Probably. And he has a right to be."

When Paige rang the doorbell, Jennifer stood behind her

and seemed to be doing her best to make herself invisible. Paige didn't blame her. She, too, was bracing herself for an outburst.

When he opened the door, there was a suspicious scowl on Ben Orcutt's face.

Paige's smile felt as if she'd glued it in place. "I'm here about your dishes, Ben. I'd like to talk to you about how I can make up for my mistake." She stepped inside the apartment, moving with some difficulty because of the tight grip Jennifer had on the back pocket of her trousers. She was half surprised that he'd invited her in instead of shutting the door in her face. "I've brought you a gift certificate for the next time you'd like Rent-A-Wife to do some work for you. And if it would make you feel better, I'd be happy to finish up the dishes again right now, just to be certain everything's satisfactory."

"They'll do," he said. His voice was cool. "I managed."

"I wouldn't dream of charging for the service today, of course. In fact, after the way my mother bullied you last night, perhaps I should offer to pay you for putting up with her."

"Spunky woman, your mother."

Paige thought it was surely the strangest adjective ever applied to Eileen McDermott. She'd heard her mother called rude, overbearing, opinionated, manipulative, domineering. But *spunky*?

"She tends to speak her mind," Paige said carefully. "She doesn't mean any harm by it."

Jennifer peeked out at him. "My daddy calls her the dragon on wheels," she offered.

Ben made a noise somewhere between a laugh and a sneeze. "Dragon on wheels—that's a good one. Is this the little girl you told me you don't have, Paige?"

"That's right," Paige said dryly.

Jennifer retreated behind her again.

"Would you like a candy bar?" Ben asked her.

Paige said, "It's almost time for dinner, Jennifer. I don't think—"

"If she's not yours," Ben said slyly, "what have you got to say about it?" He reached into a nearby dish and held out a wrapped chocolate bar that was nearly as long as Jennifer's forearm.

The child's eyes widened. She peeked up at Paige.

"Save it for after dinner, young one," Ben said. "And here, take one for the dragon—for Mrs. McDermott, too. How about you, Paige?"

A few minutes later, Paige was unlocking the minivan, her head still spinning.

"Big people are funny," Jennifer said solemnly. Clutching a gigantic candy bar in each hand, she climbed carefully into the van. "Like Mr. Orcutt."

"I couldn't agree more," Paige muttered.

"And Ms. Cade, too," Jennifer went on. "Why did she get out of breath today when you told her we were going up to the apartment to get my clothes?"

The child was right. Tricia Cade had not only had the wind knocked out of her by that announcement, she'd turned almost purple with annoyance. She'd acted, in fact, as if Paige had been purposely rubbing in the news, rather than simply informing the building super that one of her tenants would be gone for a few days.

And of course Jennifer hadn't missed that byplay. The child was frighteningly perceptive to adult nuances, Paige thought. It was just a good thing she didn't yet understand the emotions that lay beneath.

She parked her minivan beside the bungalow and leaned

across to unbuckle Jennifer's seat belt. "My mother," she said carefully, "can be a little grumpy sometimes, too."

"Like Mr. Orcutt?"

"A whole lot more so. And it wouldn't be a good idea at all to tell her what your father calls her. So do me a favor and forget that name, okay?"

Jennifer nodded, but Paige wasn't certain she'd heard. The child's attention was riveted on the back of the house, where a winter-bare lilac bush bordered the steps to the back porch. "There's the cat, Paige. I thought you said she'd have gone home."

Paige could see nothing but the shifting of a branch in the gusty wind, and she suspected that was what Jennifer had seen, too. "Any animal with sense would have." She ushered Jennifer up the steps.

For an instant, as she entered the kitchen, a sense of déjà vu gripped her. Centered on the table was a vase full of flowers —a pretty autumn-colored bouquet of mums, carnations, and lilies, surrounded with dark green foliage and with a single spray of brilliant red maple leaves to accent the arrangement. Yesterday a single rose, today a whole bouquet—

She reached for the tiny envelope which nestled almost out of sight in the greenery.

From the doorway, Eileen quoted Paige's own words back at her. "Since when do you read my cards?"

Paige almost knocked the vase over. "I'm sorry. I assumed—"

"That I'm too decrepit for anyone to send me flowers?"

"Of course not, Mother." The bouquet must be from Austin, she realized. Addressed to Eileen, the flowers must have been meant as a sort of message to Paige, as well, an assurance that he was taking his promise seriously, that he was really going to try to patch things up with Eileen.

She studied the flowers once more. Somehow, the bouquet wasn't the kind she would have expected Austin to send, though it was certainly nice enough. She couldn't quite put her finger on the difference. What had she expected? Something with more class, somehow. Something more exotic, or bigger and grander...

But then, she reminded herself, Eileen would be justifiably suspicious if her ex-son-in-law were to suddenly start sending her truckloads of orchids.

And that kind of overkill wouldn't be like Austin, either, Paige thought, remembering the classic restraint of the single pink rose he'd sent her yesterday. One rose was thoughtful, perfect, tasteful. A dozen of them would have been vulgar—out of all proportion to the favor she'd done.

"They're a piece of nonsense anyway," Eileen said gruffly. "Fresh flowers are a waste of money. A potted plant—that's a little different, because it lasts. Of course, some people have more money than is good for them, so if they want to throw it away on flowers that are just going to wilt in a day or two, I guess that's their business."

Austin, Paige thought, had his work cut out for him.

Eileen peered past Paige. "Who's that standing behind you?"

For an instant, Paige had entirely forgotten Jennifer. It was funny, she thought, how quickly one became accustomed to a small hand clinging to one's pocket flap.

She said firmly, "A houseguest who will be staying with us for a couple of days. This is Jennifer."

"Come out so I can look at you, child."

Jennifer took a cautious step forward. "I have a candy bar for you," she volunteered, and held it out.

Paige noted that in the heat of the child's hand the paper wrapper had crumpled and the chocolate had softened, so the giant bar was now shaped in a gentle curve.

"Very sweet of you." Eileen said dryly. "I'm sure that was all your own idea."

"No," Jennifer said innocently. "It was Mr. Orcutt's. He gave me one, too. Do you have legs under that blanket?"

Paige braced herself for a lecture on why little girls shouldn't ask rude questions, but her mother merely pushed aside the quilted lap cover.

Jennifer's brown eyes were wide as she surveyed Eileen, who had hunched down a little in her wheelchair. "Is that why your chair has wheels?"

"Yes, because my legs don't work very well."

"Will they get better?"

"Probably not. Do you have another name, or are you just Jennifer?"

Here we go, thought Paige.

"I'm Jennifer Weaver," the child said.

Eileen's lips pursed, and her eyes turned to ice. "So that's it."

Jennifer crept a little closer to Paige.

Paige moved quickly to take a shallow dish from the cupboard and the milk carton from a low shelf on the refrigerator door. She poured a splash of milk into the dish and held it out to Jennifer. "Maybe you can tempt the cat out of hiding," she suggested. "Put this at the bottom of the steps, and then sit at the top very quietly and watch."

Eyes alight, Jennifer dropped the chocolate bars on the kitchen table and seized the dish with both hands.

"If the cat comes out, don't try to touch it," Paige called as the child slid out the back door.

"I wouldn't hurt her." Jennifer sounded insulted at the very idea.

"I know you wouldn't, but the cat doesn't understand that. It might be wild, and it could scratch you."

Eileen sniffed. "Now we're not only taking in neglected children but we're feeding stray cats?"

Paige closed the back door. "She's not neglected. Austin had to go out of town suddenly. He had arrangements made for her, but they fell through. And I don't think there's really a cat at all. I think Jennifer saw a branch move and imagined the rest. But the activity will entertain her for a few minutes." She squared her shoulders. "While we talk."

"Not a bad idea," Eileen said. "What are you thinking of, Paige McDermott? Isn't it enough that he used you once and discarded you the moment he didn't need you anymore? Now he's back. And not only does he still seem to have all his manipulative charm, but obviously that little girl has inherited it, as well. It appears he chose his weapon well."

So much for the flowers, Paige thought. The bouquet had been a waste of time and effort; Eileen had written it off as no more than an expression of Austin's manipulative charm...

But then, Paige thought irritably, what sort of fool would think that a simple bouquet could heal years-deep wounds? No matter what he'd written on that card...

Actually, she realized, that was what had been nagging at her all along. She'd expected something better of Austin. Something more imaginative. Something more *effective*.

"How you feel about Austin is your business, Mother," she said. "I understand that you still resent him and that you feel you have good reason, but—"

"*I feel?* Like I've imagined what he did to you?"

"What he did to me is my business. In any case, you will not take out your frustrations with Austin on his daughter."

"Just don't expect me to take care of her."

"I wouldn't dream of asking."

Eileen gave a snort. "Then I'd say we've both made ourselves pretty clear."

"Good. You'll treat Jennifer like—"

"He's got you wrapped tight around his finger again, doesn't he, Paige? Throwing his daughter at you to take care of... Has he talked you back into bed yet?"

Despite her best efforts, Paige felt herself color violently. "Of course not."

Eileen's eyes narrowed. "Does that mean he hasn't tried? Or that he hasn't succeeded?"

"Neither. Not that it's your business."

"What affects my daughter's happiness is my business. I don't want you to forget what your marriage was really like. If putting my nose into things will keep you from being foolish enough to fall for that man again—"

"I'm not likely to forget, Mother. Especially as long as I have his daughter right here to remind me."

"Hmm," Eileen said. "I guess we'll see about that, won't we?"

CHAPTER SEVEN

JENNIFER was, as ordered, sitting just outside the bungalow's enclosed back porch, atop the flight of steps. Her feet were drawn up under her, and her arms hugged her knees. She looked very cold, Paige thought, and very much alone.

The child looked up with a frown as Paige crossed the porch. "You scared her away."

"Her?" Paige asked.

"The kitty. I sat here and I sat here, and finally she came out to eat, just when you opened the door."

So Jennifer had been right; there was a cat, after all. "Maybe she'll come back." Paige settled as quietly as she could onto the step.

Jennifer leaned against her.

Paige's heart squeezed painfully. *He chose his weapon well,* Eileen had said, implying that Austin was using Jennifer for his own nefarious purposes. If Paige fell in love with Jennifer...then what?

He's just trying to lure me back into bed, no doubt, Paige thought wryly, and shook her head in astonishment that her mother could truly be shortsighted enough to believe that Austin had any such intention. What on earth could he gain?

Pleasure, of course—there had never been any shortage of enjoyment in their marriage bed, and Paige didn't doubt that Austin remembered that fact just as clearly as she did. But a man in Austin's position could find feminine diversion anywhere he looked. He didn't need to chase after a woman who represented as many bad memories as good ones, one who could only complicate his life, when there were women like Tricia Cade panting to be noticed.

No, Eileen was dead wrong about that.

And she was wrong, too, that Austin had set out to insert Jennifer into Paige's life. He was simply a single parent stuck in a bad situation. Once he was home from this business trip, once the school was back in operation, once he'd had a chance to settle in and make some new friends…then he wouldn't need to rely on Paige any longer. And he'd no doubt be as relieved when that day came as she would be.

Paige would see him now and then, of course. She couldn't possibly avoid Sabrina's parties for the rest of her life, even if she wanted to, and he would no doubt be part of the crowd on occasion. She'd probably even see Jennifer now and then, at events like the Tanner Electronics Christmas party. But it wouldn't be like this.

And, she thought as she felt the trusting weight of the child against her, she'd better not forget it.

From under the lilac bush crept the scrawniest tiger-striped cat Paige had ever seen. It was hardly larger than a kitten, though it obviously wasn't just a baby but a very skinny young adult. It seemed to be all eyes, ears, and tail.

"I've never had a kitty before," Jennifer said softly.

Paige bit her tongue to keep from pointing out that the child didn't have one now, either. An emaciated, wild-eyed stray was hardly a pet. Besides, she suspected, both Austin and the management of Aspen Towers would have something to say about the subject of a cat in the penthouse apartment.

The cat's ears tipped as if to capture Jennifer's wheedling tone, and then the animal took a last slurp of milk and darted back under the porch.

"Time to come in," Paige said. "You're trembling from the cold."

"But she might come back."

"If she does, there's more milk in the dish."

"But it'll freeze!"

"Cats have ways of keeping warm."

"I mean the milk will freeze," Jennifer said impatiently.

"You can bring more out after dinner."

Jennifer's mouth set firmly, and Paige knew the battle line had been drawn. She was contemplating her next move, and thinking about how much that obstinate jaw reminded her of Austin, when Eileen opened the back door. "Phone," she said briefly.

"I'll be right there, Mother."

"It's for Jennifer."

The child's face lit up. "Daddy!" she shrieked, and the cat was forgotten as she leaped up and tore past the wheelchair and into the house.

A few minutes later, Jennifer was sitting in the middle of the kitchen floor with the cordless phone while Paige put the finishing touches on the meal Eileen had started. Much as she tried not to listen, Paige couldn't avoid hearing Jennifer's end of the conversation. Not that it did her much good; the child was practically monosyllabic. Finally, however, she held out the telephone to Paige. "Daddy wants to talk to you," she announced.

Keep it light, Paige reminded herself. "You've got great timing, Austin. This phone call got me out of a pinch here."

"With Jen or your mother?"

"Your daughter went on strike and refused to come inside."

"You're kidding. The poster girl for central heating wanted to stay out in the cold?"

"Well, she's trying to adopt a stray cat. Don't worry, it's about as approachable as a leopard in the wild." She glanced over her shoulder at Eileen, who with lips pressed tight together was laying flatware on the table, while Jennifer watched intently.

Paige took the phone around the corner into the hall. "Maybe I should release you from your promise," she said. "Mother's looking grumpy at the moment simply because she happened to answer the phone, and the flowers certainly didn't do quite what you intended to soften her up."

"What flowers?"

"The ones you—" She paused. "You didn't send flowers?"

"No. The idea occurred to me, but frankly I thought it would be a little too obvious."

"I sort of thought that myself," Paige admitted. "But— Oh, well, I guess it doesn't matter. I gave your best to Tricia Cade, by the way, when I went to your apartment to pick up Jennifer's clothes. She seemed disappointed to have missed you when you went home to pack for yourself." She added, with a tinge of maliciousness, "In fact, I got the impression Tricia would have been quite pleased to run upstairs and put your things in a bag with her own little hands."

"I'll have to remember that," Austin said pleasantly.

"Just another service Aspen Towers provides to its residents, I'm sure. I had trouble finding any jeans for Jennifer, by the way."

"That's because she doesn't have any."

Paige was momentarily nonplussed. "You mean, never?"

"No, I mean she outgrew what she had, and since she's wearing school uniforms practically every day she hasn't needed play clothes. Apart from the rebellion over the cat, are things going all right? She isn't keeping you from working?''

"Everything's just fine. How's the trip?''

Such a casual conversation, she thought. So eminently normal. An eavesdropper who didn't know the circumstances might assume they were still married, the way they were chatting—comparing notes on business, child care, wardrobes, life in general. The only thing missing was the seductive nonsense he used to murmur into her ear.

And why was she thinking of things like that?

Because, Paige realized, that was almost exactly what he was doing. The subject matter was different, of course, but the tone of Austin's voice was all the reminder she needed. The mere thought made her muscles tighten.

What was it, she wondered, which made a man's voice grow sexier when it was disembodied? Austin's, for instance, was always low and deep and warm—except, of course, when he was furious—but somehow on the telephone it was even more so. How paradoxical it was that his voice was even more intimate when he was far away than if he was in the room.

As she listened to a swift assessment of Tanner's situation, she moved aside for Eileen and Jennifer as they went to wash up, and when he was finished, she didn't comment. Abruptly, she said, "Is there anything else, Austin?''

The sudden silence on the other end of the line made her realize how taut her voice suddenly sounded, and she tried to pass it off as unintentional. "It's just that dinner's getting cold, so unless there was something you needed to tell me—''

"You might let the school know where Jennifer's staying.''

"In case they open again sooner than expected? I already have."

"That's the only thing I can think of." Austin was studiously polite. "May I call again tomorrow?"

"Of course. I'll tell Jennifer to expect it." *And that should make it plain that I don't have any illusions about this easy chatter leading anywhere.*

She carried the hot casserole dish across the kitchen and stood eyeing the bouquet which Eileen had moved to one end of the table.

It would be unforgivably nosy to peek at that card, she told herself. But the question, like an allergic rash, gave her no peace. If Austin hadn't sent the flowers, who had?

She heard the quiet swish of Eileen's wheelchair and stepped away from the table, though it wasn't her mother's approach which had made her squash the temptation to pry. And much as she'd like to, Paige couldn't pretend that it was good old-fashioned conscience which had stopped her, either.

What had really made her hand drop away from the flowers was the simple fact that the card was no longer there. Eileen must have removed it, along with the mail, while she was setting the table.

At the deli where the partners met for lunch each Wednesday, the usual crowd was waiting in line. In the choicest corner booth, Cassie and Sabrina were already deep in conversation, the curly red head and the sleek dark one close together. Paige set her tray down on the table and handed Jennifer the basket containing her sandwich and chips.

"Sorry you've had to wait for us," Paige said sweetly.

"No need to apologize," Sabrina said. "You're right on time."

"Really? Then you must have been very early, to snag

this booth. Have I missed much of the conversation?''
Paige thought Cassie looked a little chagrined, which only
confirmed her suspicion that the subject of the conversation had been Paige herself, and the early meeting deliberate.

"We were just discussing Ben Orcutt," Sabrina said
airily. "He called Cassie this morning."

"He can't possibly be out of clean dishes already."
Paige took a bite from her turkey sandwich. "So does he
need his checkbook balanced, a couple of buttons sewed
on, or his refrigerator cleaned out?"

"He never mentioned dishes, checkbooks, or buttons,"
Cassie said. "And his refrigerator hasn't been too bad ever
since Sabrina taught him the fine art of putting leftovers
down the garbage disposal instead of stashing them till
they turn into antibiotics. I didn't even have to throw away
my rubber gloves after the last time I cleaned it."

"Then what did he want?" Paige asked.

Cassie toyed with her soda. "He told me he has a Rent-A-Wife gift certificate he wants to spend—but where he'd
have gotten that is beyond me."

"Especially," Sabrina chimed in, "since we don't have
them. Not that gift certificates are a bad idea, but—"

Paige used her forefinger to gather up a few stray bread
crumbs. "I was going to mention it. I thought, with the
holiday coming up, it might be a good promotion. So I
designed a certificate—"

"But where did Ben get hold of one?"

Paige very carefully rubbed the crumbs from her fingertip, letting them drop into a discarded paper napkin. "I
gave it to him as a sort of bonus. I was trying not to lose
a client."

Sabrina's eyebrows soared. Cassie said, "Lose *Ben?*
How in heaven's name could we do that?"

Jennifer, who had been looking around the deli and apparently paying no attention to the conversation, said suddenly, "He was mad at Paige. At least she said he was, but he didn't look mad to me."

"Thank you very much for that clarification, Jennifer," Paige said. "It's a long story, and since I think I have the trouble smoothed over, why go into the details? So why did he call you about the gift certificate, Cassie?"

"Because he's obviously still mad at you, and he's too smart to call me," Sabrina said irrepressibly, "since he wants someone to cook for him."

"Better judgment than I expected from Ben," Paige agreed. "But he gets most of his meals delivered from the senior citizen service, doesn't he?"

Sabrina shrugged. "Maybe he's tired of their menus."

"Or maybe he's taking my advice and inviting the neighbors in for cards and snacks."

"He's not quite sure what he wants," Cassie said. "And it was no fun trying to pin him down."

Sabrina's eyes lighted. "Maybe he's in love! Dinner for two, candlelight—"

"Perhaps that's why he wasn't furious with me, after all," Paige mused. "If he was thinking about his party instead of the way I messed up—"

Cassie and Sabrina exchanged a look, and Sabrina said, "Look out the window, Jennifer—it's started to snow. Are you finished with your sandwich? Let's go out, and I'll teach you to catch snowflakes on your tongue."

"Don't be long," Paige said. "Remember we have to make a quick stop for cat food, Jennifer."

"Cat food? Who's that for?" Sabrina asked.

Jennifer looked at her as if she'd slipped a cog. "My cat."

Cassie said, "I thought the leases at Aspen Towers don't allow pets."

"I'm sure they don't." Paige pushed her sandwich aside. "But this is not an ordinary pet, believe me." She waited till the two were out of hearing range. "Go ahead, Cassie. By the way, how did you and Sabrina decide which one of you would distract Jennifer and which would have a little chat with me? Did you draw the short straw?"

Cassie sighed. "We're just concerned, Sabrina and me. You've been acting really strangely lately."

"You're right. It's not like me to offend a client. I can only say that I've had a lot on my mind lately, and—"

"A lot? Are you sure it's not just one specific thing that's causing the trouble, Paige?"

"You mean Jennifer?"

"No, I mean Jennifer's daddy. For a woman who just a few weeks ago didn't want to have anything to do with Austin Weaver when he came to town for his interview, you certainly have got chummy with him in a hurry."

"Who says I want to have anything to do with him now? I didn't ask for this complication in my life."

"Didn't you? You didn't have to take on Jennifer. You could have told him to call Sabrina or me."

Paige blinked. It was a perfectly sensible option; why, she wondered, hadn't it occurred to her? She said defensively, "Sabrina's wedding is less than two weeks off and you're up to your ears in work."

"So are you," Cassie reminded. "I'm worried about you, Paige. You're the most home-minded of all three of us, and despite your attitude about men, I suspect you're the most susceptible. Especially where there's a child concerned—and a child who could clearly use a mom, at that."

"Cassie—"

"Honey, for a guy who's got a kid, Austin isn't exactly the most domesticated creature I've ever encountered. And his track record isn't very good, either."

Paige shrugged. "It's not his fault Jennifer's mother died."

Cassie's eyes widened. "What? Is that what he told you? He's divorced, Paige. His employment paperwork says so."

Oops, Paige thought.

But that made no sense. Why would Austin have mentioned his failed marriage? There would have been no need to list anything but his current, official marital status.

Cassie's voice was taut. "If he told you he's a widower—"

"Jennifer did. She told Sabrina, too, as a matter of fact," Paige added almost triumphantly. "And when she announced that her mother had died, Austin was right there."

"That's odd." Cassie bit her lip. "I suppose it's possible she died after they were divorced, and rather than upset the child unnecessarily by going into detail..."

"Does it matter, Cassie?" Paige pushed her sandwich aside. "Anyway, how do you know what's in his personnel file? Those things are supposed to be confidential."

Cassie had the grace to color a little. "Jake let it slip. He's worried about you, too, Paige. If Austin isn't telling you the truth—"

Paige took a deep breath. She'd let this go on too long, hoping it wouldn't be necessary to ever confess what an idiot she'd been. But she couldn't lie to her partners, even by omission, any longer. "As long as we're talking about truth, Cassie—"

Before she could gather her courage, Jennifer burst through the door and came to a screeching halt beside the booth, holding out both mittens to display the enormous snowflakes which had caught against the bright red wool. "Look, Paige!"

"I see, darling. How wonderful." She couldn't confess now, of course, with Jennifer listening in; if the child was ever to know of her father's marital misadventure, the news would have to come directly from him. Paige, guiltily aware of a tinge of relief because of the reprieve, looked straight at Cassie over the child's head and said, "Don't worry, I won't get confused. And believe me, I'm not in the least susceptible where Austin's concerned."

Cassie, she thought, did not look convinced.

The snow fell heavily for the rest of the afternoon, as if Mother Nature was setting out to clothe the city for Christmas. Jennifer was ecstatic; Paige was torn between enjoying the child's excitement and being annoyed at how the weather impacted her job. Every errand took twice as long, with the streets clogged by snow and slow-moving traffic. And every senior citizen on the client list seemed to be calling for extra help because of the storm.

When Sabrina had first suggested adding another partner to Rent-A-Wife, Paige hadn't taken her too seriously. But she thought now that perhaps she'd been a little too quick to dismiss the notion. One more set of hands would come in very handy indeed, and not only when the first real storm of winter set in. Not only was Rent-A-Wife growing, but the pressures on the three of them were increasing at an even faster rate than the business was.

It had been different when all of them were single, able to arrange their lives around the job and willing to work extreme hours some days because they knew other days would be correspondingly relaxed. But now Cassie was a wife for real, and Sabrina soon would be—and they had other demands on their time. Paige couldn't blame them for wanting their working hours to be more predictable, or for wanting their evenings and weekends free.

Besides, those additional demands would only increase as time went on, especially as they started families. It simply wasn't possible to explain to a hungry baby that mealtime would be late because Mom had to run just one more errand.

Only Paige was still in the same circumstances as when they had originally set up the business. Only Paige was still on her own, with no one but Eileen...

Quit feeling sorry for yourself, she ordered. *You're perfectly content. You're doing exactly what you want to do.*

She glanced in the mirror at Jennifer, who was securely belted into the minivan's back seat, singing Christmas carols to herself. The child broke off in midphrase. "I read a story once about a snowman. Can we build one when we get home?"

Home, Paige thought. It was such a careless word, under these circumstances. Meaningless, really. To Jennifer it merely signified their immediate destination, not a permanent location.

"We're late," Paige temporized. "And your daddy will be calling."

"Eileen will answer the phone. She's not really a dragon, after all. So we *can* build a snowman."

"Maybe after dinner."

"But then it'll be dark!" Jennifer wailed.

As Paige swung the van into the bungalow's driveway, the tires started to slide on the packed-down snow at the precise moment she realized that a car was already parked in the space where the minivan usually sat. She fought the van to a halt just inches from the back bumper of a black Jaguar and sagged thankfully against the steering wheel.

Jennifer bounced madly in her seat till Paige opened the door, and then—snowman forgotten—she was off at full speed. Paige followed, wondering how long Austin had been there, waiting for them. Not long, surely, or Eileen would have phoned her. Unless she'd been too busy giving Austin a very large piece of her mind...

But the living room didn't resemble a bloody battlefield, as Paige had half expected, though the atmosphere was certainly tense. She could feel the strain as soon as she stepped into the room, even though there was no obvious reason for it. In fact, she thought ironically, it looked like a perfect domestic scene.

Jennifer was already in her father's arms, being swung high for a hug. Eileen was sitting in her favorite spot, next to the work table which held her sewing supplies, with a half-quilted throw across her lap and her needle poised for the next stitch. But her gaze wasn't quite focused on the fabric; she looked, Paige thought, as if she'd stuck a finger in an electrical socket. But then, that would be precisely the effect of unexpectedly finding her ex-son-in-law on her doorstep.

"I didn't think you'd be back till tomorrow," Paige said. "In fact, with the condition the streets are in, I'm surprised the airport's open."

"Barely," Austin said. "If Caleb hadn't chartered a jet we'd still be stuck in California."

Jennifer was struggling to get down. "I have to go feed my kitty," she announced. "And build a snowman. Come help, Daddy."

Paige intervened. "Honey, your daddy must be anxious to get home and have you all to himself."

"And Paige," Austin told the child, "must be anxious to have a little time without you so she can do whatever she wants."

Jennifer skewered Paige with a look. "You want me to go away?"

"Of course not," Paige said. "But—"

"I'm not in a hurry," Austin admitted.

Eileen tossed her quilting aside. "So go build a snowman already," she muttered. "It'll take a while to finish dinner, anyway. I'll call you in."

Jennifer let out a whoop and headed for the door, doing her best to drag Austin with her.

Paige, openmouthed, stood in the center of the living room and stared at her mother.

"Good thing it's not mosquito season," Eileen said irritably, "or you'd have swallowed a quart of them by now."

"Did I hear you invite Austin to dinner?"

"Not precisely. I figure since I've already started cooking, Jennifer might as well have a good meal before she goes home." Eileen spun her wheelchair toward the kitchen door, muttering under her breath. "Heaven knows what he'd feed her. Gone for days on end, there's probably nothing in the refrigerator—"

Paige rubbed her temples and followed. So much for the electrical shock her mother had gotten, she thought. Paige herself felt as if she'd been struck by lightning.

Jennifer was coming inside again with the margarine tub which had become the stray cat's designated dinner bowl. "Daddy's going to catch my kitty," she announced.

"The idiot will get himself scratched." Paige flung herself across the enclosed back porch and stopped dead just outside the door.

Crouched at the base of the steps, Austin was holding out one hand. And Jennifer's very wild, very stray, very scrawny cat was sniffing his fingers.

"That answers one question for certain," Paige muttered. "Jen's instinct was right—that creature *is* a female."

Austin looked up with a smile which lighted his face and made Paige feel as if the step under her feet had suddenly turned into a merry-go-round.

Jennifer squeezed past her and stood wide-eyed.

"Come down slowly, Jen," Austin said softly.

Within a couple of minutes, the cat was sampling the contents of the dish while with one finger Jennifer stroked the animal's back.

"Now I can take her home with me," the child breathed.

Austin winced.

Paige bit her lip in a futile effort to keep from smiling. "Oh, great animal tamer," she said under her breath. "How are you going to get yourself out of this one?"

"Touching her is one thing," Austin said. "Picking her up and stuffing her in your backpack is something else altogether. I don't think she'd like it at all."

"To say nothing of having to fumigate the backpack afterward to get rid of the vermin who would no doubt come along for the ride," Paige added. She brushed snow off the bottom step and sat down.

"But if I go home without my kitty, who will feed her?" Realization had obviously hit Jennifer like a hammer; her tone was tragic.

Paige smothered a sigh. Of course, she'd known from the first bowl of milk that she was doomed to end up with a cat; she just hadn't wanted to admit it. "I will. And you can come and visit her anytime—" An instant too late, she saw the speculative tilt of Austin's head. Was he wondering about her reasons for that invitation? "Anytime your father says you can," she added lamely.

The cat slurped up the last bite of food, leaving the dish

as spotless as if it had just come out of the dishwasher, and retreated under the porch. Jennifer said, "Daddy, make her come back."

Austin rose from his crouched position. "I can't. Why don't you build a snow cat, instead of a snowman? Maybe she'll come out to look at that." He sat down on the opposite end of the step from Paige.

She didn't look at him but at Jennifer, already plunging through a snowbank. "She'll soon forget all about the cat, I'm sure. And there are all kinds of reasons why she can't come to visit, so—"

"Including that you'd rather not be bothered?"

His voice was so matter of fact that it took a moment for his meaning to sink in, and when it did, Paige was stunned. "Of course that's not what I meant! I've enjoyed having her here."

"Then what did you mean?"

She stretched one foot out and drew lines in the snow with the toe of her boot. "I'd prefer you didn't get the idea that I want you to bring her," she said slowly.

"I see. It's me you'd rather not be bothered with."

"I can't imagine that wounding your self-esteem, Austin."

"Can't you? You requested that I make peace with your mother, and I think I've made considerable progress."

"I'm flabbergasted," Paige said frankly.

"So what about you, Paige? You're the one who said you didn't want to be caught in a war."

"I don't. But there's a considerable difference between calling a truce and forming an alliance."

Austin's dark eyebrows rose. "Are you suggesting that we form an alliance?"

Paige could have bitten her tongue off. "Of course not,"

she said crossly. "This is why I don't want to talk to you, Austin. You're always twisting what I say."

"Maybe I just need practice."

"No, you're already plenty good at it."

"Now who's twisting words?" he said mildly. "I'd like to take you to dinner, Paige."

She shook her head. "I don't think that's a good idea. Jennifer will want to spend your first evening at home with you. And you'd sacrifice all the ground you won with Mother, too. After she's actually invited you…"

"I didn't mean tonight. Eight o'clock tomorrow?"

Paige chewed her lower lip. "You mean this as a way to thank me for taking care of Jennifer, of course."

Austin shrugged. "If that's what you want to call it." He let the silence stretch. "If your mother can bend, Paige, why won't you give it a try?"

"Why are you doing this?"

"Unfinished business," he said. "You're right, you know, that we're going to run into each other, but surely there's no need for us to be uncomfortable about it. Obviously we can't just ignore the past, though. We've been trying to do that and it isn't working very well. So we need to deal with it. Mend the fences and move on."

"And you think having dinner together will do that."

"It can't be worse than we're doing now, can it?"

Paige couldn't argue with that. And she could hardly refuse.

It was, after all, such a reasonable thing to ask. How could she possibly turn down such a practical, sensible, *nice* request? If she did, she'd look as if she was scared to death of him.

Which, of course, she was. But truth was no help right now.

"All right," she said. "Eight o'clock tomorrow."

Because, after all—what else could she say?

CHAPTER EIGHT

FOR the life of her, Paige couldn't think of anything sensible to say to break the silence. She looked out across the lawn to where Jennifer was bent almost double as she tried in vain to lift the giant snowball she'd rolled, and went to assist her.

Just as she leaned over to help the child, Jennifer stood up and the top of her head cracked against Paige's chin, catching her lower lip between her teeth. The pain brought hot tears to Paige's eyes, and when she tentatively touched her lip, her finger came away red.

Jennifer's eyes were wide. "I'm sorry," she gasped. "I'll go get you a bandage."

Austin's long strides brought him across the snow-covered lawn to Paige, and he gently tugged her hand away so he could check the damage. "A bandage wouldn't do any good, Jen," he said. He bent to scoop up a handful of snow, pressing it against the wounded lip.

Paige winced at the cold. "You'll freeze your hand," she said, trying not to move her lips.

"Don't try to talk," Austin ordered. "You're not a very good ventriloquist anyway. I can't understand you."

"It will, too, help," Jennifer announced. "I *always* feel better with a bandage." She darted off toward the house.

"The answer to all childhood woes," Austin said. His voice took on the singsong note of a carnival barker. "Scraped knee? Chicken pox? Compound fracture of the leg? Just slap an adhesive bandage on it—preferably a sparkly orange one—and it'll feel better instantly."

Paige started to smile as she looked up at him, but she stopped when she saw the glow in his eyes, just inches above her face. She swallowed convulsively.

Austin sobered. "I'm sorry, I shouldn't try to make you laugh. Stretching your lip will hurt and make it start to bleed again."

A drip of melted snow rolled down Paige's throat, drawing an icy line across the tender skin, through the gap where she had neglected to button her coat collar, and straight down into her cleavage. She gasped and tried to pull away, clutching at the errant water drop.

Austin held the snow pack even more firmly against her mouth, and with his other hand he scooped up the next wandering droplet before it could reach the base of her throat. Paige supposed she should be grateful for his quick action, but in fact where his fingertips had brushed, her skin burned even worse than her injured lip did.

Austin lifted the packed snow away to inspect the cut. "I think it's stopped now." He gently touched the spot with the tip of his finger.

Despite the numbing cold, his touch was like a hot rivet holding Paige in place. She stared up at him and watched as his eyes narrowed and went dark. Ever so slowly his hand slipped from her mouth to her throat to the back of her neck, his fingers spreading over the soft skin to hold her, and he lowered his head.

Just as his lips brushed hers, the slam of the back door jolted Paige out of her paralysis. By the time Jennifer skidded to a stop in the snow next to them, they were standing two feet apart. Austin was still holding the reddened, icy clump of snow, but he looked as if he'd forgotten it entirely.

"I brought you a bandage, Paige," Jennifer said breath-lessly. "Was Daddy kissing your hurt lip to make it all better?"

Austin gave a gasp of laughter.

From the back door, Eileen called them to dinner. Paige wondered how much she'd seen, and what she'd have to say about it.

"I don't want dinner," Jennifer called back. "I'm not hungry, and my snow cat's not done."

"No dinner," Paige said, "means no hot chocolate afterward."

Jennifer eyed her for a moment. "Can I have it in one of the special cups?"

Paige nodded, and the child spun toward the house and took off at a dead run.

More slowly, Austin and Paige waded back to the edge of the driveway. As she carefully watched her step in the icy spots where the minivan's tires had packed down the snow, Paige caught a glimpse of Austin's elegant wingtips. "Thanks for the first aid," she said. "But your shoes are soaked from standing in the snow."

"They'll dry." As soon as he was inside the back door he kicked his shoes off. "You must have bought Jennifer's boots," he said. "Thanks, Paige. She didn't need them in Atlanta, and I haven't had time since we got here."

His voice was just a little husky, and it made Paige feel almost ticklish. She tried to defend herself from the sensation by saying lightly, "I'll make sure you get the bill."

Eileen's shepherd's pie sat steaming in the center of the kitchen table, and Jennifer was already in her customary place. She waited only till the adults were seated before she announced, "Daddy, I'm going to name my cat Fluffy."

Paige couldn't think of a less appropriate name for a scrawny cat whose coat was so patchy it was practically threadbare. She sent a sidelong glance at Austin; seeing his barely repressed grin made it even harder to hold in her own enjoyment. "Jennifer," she murmured, "you have a career in fiction waiting for you."

"Or marketing," Austin added. "No, I've got it. Public relations—that's your field, Jen. The fine art of making people who are looking at something believe wholeheartedly that it's something else altogether."

Jennifer looked from one to the other, eyes wide in puzzlement.

"Now that all of you are quite finished," Eileen said austerely, "let's link hands around the table and say grace, before dinner gets cold."

It's only for a moment, Paige told herself. *It's not like holding hands to walk down the street.* It wasn't at all the same thing they used to do. Nevertheless it was with trepidation that she laid her fingers against Austin's open palm.

His hand was as warm as if he'd never held a snowball, and his hold was casual. Paige closed her eyes and let the soft ritual words wash over her. But she didn't really hear them; her entire consciousness was focused on the feel of her hand against Austin's.

This, she thought, *is how it should have been.* Casually gathered together, shoes kicked off, for a family dinner following a romp in the snow. Three generations clasping hands and giving thanks, sharing and teasing and laughing... This was how it could have been. Jennifer could have been her daughter, and at the end of the day the three of them could have gone home together. They could have been a real family...

Eileen finished saying grace, but Austin didn't let Paige's hand slip from his. Instead, he looked from her fingertips to Jennifer's, clasped in his other hand. "I see you two have the same manicurist."

Paige could feel herself flush as red as the smudged scarlet polish on her nails. "It was the only thing that kept Jennifer entertained this afternoon while we had a long wait."

He looked at her, Paige thought, a little oddly. But all he said was, "In that case, thank heaven I wasn't the one who had to wait with her."

He released her hand. And just as easily, Paige thought, he had dismissed her from his mind.

A real family. Except, Paige reminded herself harshly, that Austin hadn't wanted it to be that way. So he had walked out on Paige and married Marliss Howard instead, and given her his daughter.

And there was no point at all in feeling sentimental over the old days. All that had been nothing more than illusion.

Paige looked down at her plate and was mildly surprised to see it full of shepherd's pie and salad, for she couldn't remember spooning up her portions. With deliberate coolness she asked, "Austin, what will you do with Jennifer tomorrow while you go to work?"

Eileen said, "I forgot to tell you, didn't I? There's a message in your stack. The academy will be back in session tomorrow."

"You forgot to tell me?" Paige asked skeptically.

"Once I'd told Austin, I didn't think it was terribly important to inform you." Eileen's voice was tart.

Because Jennifer's schooling isn't my business, Paige thought. Admitting the fact was like scraping her fingernails across the surface of the pretty—and false—picture she'd so carefully constructed a few minutes ago.

"Do I have to go to school, Daddy?" Jennifer stirred her shepherd's pie. "I have fun with Paige."

Before Austin could answer, Eileen asked, "What did you do today?"

Jennifer bounced a little in her chair. "We took a dog to have his hair cut. And we went to a really neat store and I wanted to buy—"

"Everything she saw," Paige put in. "It was the Salvation Army thrift shop, and she said she'd never been anyplace like it before."

"I shouldn't think so," Austin muttered. "I suppose that's where the nail polish came from?"

"And then we went to the tire place and waited for a long time." Jennifer sighed at the memory. "But they had a television so it was all right. I watched cartoons and painted Paige's fingernails."

"Not that many cartoons," Paige said. "And that's no way to impress your father, Jennifer. You might tell him about the books we read."

"In between cartoons. And we went to see Mr. Orcutt," Jennifer finished triumphantly. "He gave me a peanut butter cup this time but I ate it already because we went right after lunch."

Eileen's eyes narrowed. "I thought you were just there yesterday, Paige. You're surely not still trying to win him back, are you?"

Paige shifted uneasily and wished Jennifer hadn't gone into quite such detail. "A little customer relations work—"

"We took him cookies," Jennifer put in. "I'm done with my dinner. Can I have my hot chocolate now?"

"It's getting late, Jen," Austin said. "With school tomorrow—"

Jennifer's accusing eyes focused on Paige. "But you promised!"

"Yes, I did," Paige admitted. "And I shouldn't have. I'm sorry, Jennifer. I didn't know about school when I said that."

Eileen glanced at the kitchen clock. "Time does get away. If you leave right now, Austin, Jennifer will be asleep by the time you drive across town. Better give her a bath here first. Then she can ride home in her pajamas and be all ready for bed."

"That's very thoughtful, Eileen," Austin said.

Eileen's voice was brisk. "Just so we're clear about this, Austin, it's not you I'm being thoughtful of, it's Jennifer. You make the hot chocolate, Paige, while I run a bath."

She wheeled out of the room without waiting for an answer, Jennifer dancing along beside her.

Without looking at Austin, Paige reached into a box on the counter and unwrapped a china cup and saucer.

"'One of the special cups,'" Austin quoted thoughtfully. "That's the famous wedding china, isn't it? I didn't realize how literal Jen was being."

"Oh, it's not that special, really." Paige tried to keep her tone casual. "It was packed away, just taking up space in the attic, till a friend borrowed it recently. I haven't had time to put it back yet. But Jennifer likes it." She got the milk out of the refrigerator.

"I can't begin to repay you," Austin said. "Either of you. Eileen is...surprising."

"Maybe you should take Mother to dinner," Paige said carelessly.

"Too? Or instead?"

Instead. The word almost sprang to her lips before Paige paused with the milk carton suspended. "Actually, I think we should cancel the whole idea. Thanks aren't necessary, you know. Jennifer's a dear and we've enjoyed having her here."

"But that's not your real reason for backing out. Is it, Paige?" Austin moved across the room to stand beside her. "You're afraid I might try again to kiss you."

"No," she said. "I think you have a whole lot more sense than to do that."

He was right about one thing, she realized. She was afraid; part of her was scared of the consequences if she spent an entire evening alone with him.

The trouble was, the other part of her actually wanted to go. And that, in its own way, was even more frightening.

It was well past Jennifer's bedtime when they got home, and Eileen's prediction had proved accurate. The child barely stirred when Austin lifted her out of the car in front of Aspen Towers; she turned her head and buried her face in his neck as he waited for the elevator.

She smelled like vanilla, he thought. Just like Paige.

He wondered if the scent had come from Paige's shampoo or Paige herself. Jennifer had certainly hugged the woman hard enough, before they left the bungalow, to absorb any perfume or lotion Paige had been wearing; the child wouldn't have had to put it on directly.

Vanilla. Of course, Paige would wear something that smelled down to earth and domestic. No Midnight Passion kind of scents for her. If they made a perfume called Sugar Cookie, he thought wryly, Paige would probably stand in line to buy it. Not because she was trying to intrigue a man—any man—but for precisely the opposite reasons. And because she'd think it fit with Rent-A-Wife's reputation.

But what she obviously didn't realize, Austin thought, was that her carefully cultivated image, complete with the scent of vanilla, might not be as soothingly maternal as she intended it to be. Her attitude of aloofness, combined with a body curvaceous enough to make a man's palms itch, a mouth that begged to be kissed, and skin that dared him to test whether it really felt like velvet... Paige presented a challenge that some men simply wouldn't be able to resist.

Catering to male customers, going in and out of their homes, taking care of their clothes, their dogs, their cars... What else might they expect? Didn't the woman have a clue what kind of explosives she was playing with?

What was it Eileen had said tonight about one of Paige's clients? Something about trying to win him back. What if she overdid the customer relations bit and left him expecting much, much more?

If she ever looked at one of her customers as she'd looked at him tonight out in the snow—a shy upward glance through startlingly dark peek-a-boo eyelashes, with a tiny convulsive swallow and the very tip of her tongue touching the injured spot on her lip...

Across the hall from the elevator lobby, the door of the super's office was open, and Tricia Cade looked up from the papers spread across her desk and got quickly to her feet. "Austin, how nice to have you home!"

"You're here late tonight."

"Oh, you know how it is—work never seems to be done. Can I help you with anything? She looks awfully heavy."

"And it's dead weight, when she's asleep. I had to leave my bag in the car. I was hoping the doorman would still be on duty, but—"

"I'll bring it up myself," Tricia said promptly, and held out a hand for his keys. "And your mail, too—there was an overflow that wouldn't fit in the box."

Trust Tricia not to miss an opportunity, he thought.

He didn't remember till he was on the penthouse floor that his apartment key was on the same ring with those for the car. He sighed and leaned against the wall beside his door, shifting Jennifer's weight to one hip. She muttered something, then settled back against his shoulder.

His arms were aching and he was cursing Tricia under his breath by the time the elevator door opened once more and she came toward him, a bright smile on her face, his suitcase and a big plastic bag full of envelopes and magazines on an Aspen Towers' luggage cart by her side, and a ribbon-bedecked bottle cradled in one arm.

"Why are you standing out here?" she asked. "Is something wrong?"

"Would you mind unlocking the door? My arms are getting numb."

"You mean you're locked out? And I kept you waiting all this time because I had the key? I'm so sorry." She flicked expertly through his key ring. "I thought perhaps you'd like a drink, to wind down. That's what took me so long." She pushed open the door and held up the bottle as she stepped inside. "This was a gift from a grateful tenant. I thought perhaps you might like to help me drink it. It's a prize-winning wine, you know."

Austin didn't even glance at the label. "Thanks, Tricia. It's very thoughtful of you. But I really am too tired to be good company."

Tricia's smile slipped, but only for an instant. "You could never be anything but good company, Austin." Her voice was low and suggestive. She stepped a little closer.

Jennifer opened her eyes, winced at the light, and gave one pathetically tired little sob.

He had to give the woman credit; Tricia knew when she was beaten. "Perhaps another time," she said wryly. "Just shove the luggage cart out in the hall when you're done with it, and I'll have the handyman pick it up in the morning." She made a show of pulling the front door tight behind her.

"You're better than a bodyguard, Jen," Austin told the child. "You can not only spot a feint in your sleep, but you can fight it off."

He carried Jennifer down the hall to her room and tucked her in. Her hand fell nervelessly against the satin coverlet, her fingernails forming blood-red spots against the pale yellow gingham. That would have to go before school in the morning, he noted. The academy frowned on wild nail polish, especially on five-year-olds.

Funny, he thought. He'd have expected Paige to frown on it, too. He certainly wouldn't have expected her to sit still while a five-year-old painted her nails.

Jennifer sighed and yawned and half opened her eyes, holding her arms up for a final good-night hug.

"Can I bring my kitty home, Daddy?" she murmured.

"Not to the apartment, sweetheart. The lease won't allow it."

She yawned hugely. "We could just go and live with Paige." The last word was half lost as she dozed off.

Austin practically fell into bed himself, but he lay for a long time staring at the ceiling.

The irony of the situation would have appealed to his sense of humor, if only he hadn't been the one caught in the middle of it.

One woman so eager for his attention that she threw herself at him, bottle in hand... It had actually been a very clever move on Tricia's part, he thought. For one thing, the wine would have had to be chilled, and he had no doubt that Tricia had plans for the time that would have taken. It was lucky, after all, that he'd gotten to his door without a key; if he hadn't had Jennifer in his arms, providing a sort of body armor, Tricia would probably have been much more difficult to dislodge.

And another woman, so indifferent to him that the idea of him initiating a kiss had horrified her....

No, he thought. It hadn't been indifference which had made Paige shy away from his touch. And he didn't think it was distaste, either, which had made her shiver as he'd leaned down to kiss her. It was the same fear he'd seen in her eyes in his office the day he'd left town. But he still didn't know why she was afraid of him.

Was it because he was the only man on earth who knew—absolutely knew—that underneath the aloof and serene image she cultivated with such care, Paige McDermott was anything but chilly?

Or...*was* he the only one who knew that? What about that client she was so eager to keep?

The very thought annoyed him. Not because there might have been another man somewhere in her life, he assured himself. But because he was wasting perfectly good sleeping time thinking about it.

When Paige came downstairs a few minutes before eight o'clock, Eileen was sitting in her favorite chair, her quilting lying motionless in her lap. The television set was turned on but the sound was muted, and a glance showed Paige that despite Eileen's apparent absorption she probably wasn't watching, either.

At least, she thought dryly, her mother had never before shown fascination in the weather report for southwestern Asia—so no doubt what she was really doing was rehearsing a lecture on all the reasons Paige should cancel her plans for the evening. What she would never believe was that Paige not only agreed but could add a few arguments of her own.

"Did I hear the phone a few minutes ago?" Paige asked.

Eileen blinked and sat up straighter. "Sabrina called, but

she said she just wanted to gossip so she'd catch you later.''

Her eyes were brighter than usual, Paige saw, and her cheeks were a little more flushed. "Did she call twice? I thought I heard it ring again." Paige frowned. "Mother, are you running a bit of a fever?" She put out a hand to touch Eileen's forehead just as the doorbell rang.

Eileen leaned away. "What would be unusual about that? Answer the bell, Paige."

"But if you're not feeling well—"

"I'm as well as can be expected. And if you think I'm going to invite Austin Weaver to look down his nose at me by complaining about how I feel, you're wrong."

Paige sighed and opened the door. It had been such a great idea, getting Austin and Eileen to declare a truce— if it had only worked.

On the way across town, Austin said, "I hope the Pinnacle is all right with you. I asked Caleb for a recommendation, and he told me it's the best restaurant in Denver."

"Caleb thinks it's the *only* restaurant in Denver. He has breakfast there at least five days a week—and I hope he plans to keep it up after the wedding because Sabrina can't make toast without burning it."

"I didn't know they opened before lunch."

"They don't," Paige said. "They let Caleb in the back door, he sits in the kitchen, and the chef waits on him personally."

Austin grinned. "No wonder he said it would be better if he called to reserve a table for us."

Us. The nonchalant use of the word left an odd hollow in Paige's stomach. She scolded herself for even noticing, because it was so apparent that the word was meaningless to Austin. Not only weren't they still a combination, but they never had been, really. Even in the old days, when they had lived together, slept together, made love together—

How was it possible that she could have believed she knew his every thought as well as she knew every inch of his body—and been so wrong?

"You're very quiet," Austin said.

She caught her breath. "Oh, it's just that I hope you don't have vertigo. Caleb likes the tables right on the edge, where you can look straight down at the city as the restaurant revolves." She knew she sounded a little breathless—but if she was lucky, he'd think she merely had a tendency to vertigo herself. Hastily, she added, "What's Jennifer doing tonight?"

"A teenager who lives downstairs is looking after her. It turns out the super has a list."

"I bet it tightened Tricia's jaw to have to find a sitter for you," Paige mused. "I'm surprised she didn't offer to do it herself. Unless perhaps she didn't want to find out what time you got home." She intercepted his look and added with a brittle undertone, "Don't take that as any sort of invitation."

"I'm amazed," Austin murmured, "that you think I might."

Paige bit her lip hard all the rest of the way downtown.

The maître d' showed them to the closest thing to an isolated corner that the Pinnacle possessed, a table on the lowest and outermost ring of the restaurant floor. It was tucked against a wall on one side, screened by palms on the other, but it still boasted the same gorgeous view of the city. The winter darkness had closed in long since, and below them, beyond the towers of the central city, lay a golden web of lights stretching as far as they could see.

The restaurant was busy, but from their table only the murmur of distant voices, the clink of silver and china, and the occasional pop of a cork reminded them they were not alone. Austin dealt with the wine steward, and when they each had been served and the bottle was propped at an artistic angle in the silver cooler at his elbow, he raised his glass in a silent salute.

Paige turned the stemmed glass between her fingers, trying not to remember other evenings and other places—times when what they ate and drank wasn't important, simply because they were together.

At least, she thought sadly, that had been true for her.

As if he had read her mind, Austin murmured, "This isn't much like the nights we walked to the ice cream stand."

Pain shot through her, and it took all Paige's self-control to joke, "Not at all. Back then, we were looking up instead of down, and the golden flecks we saw in the sky were insects flying into the streetlights."

He smiled, but his eyes didn't join in the humor. "You don't want to remember, do you?"

"I don't see any point in it."

"I wanted to do this for you then, Paige." He leaned forward, and his sun-browned hand came to rest very gently on hers as it lay on the table. "I would like to do it for you now. I don't mean dinner. I mean…life."

A muffled gasp above her head drew Paige's attention to the upper level of the restaurant, to the one place where an onlooker could see them. She caught only a glimpse of long black hair and exotically slanted green eyes before the woman drew back out of sight, but it was enough.

Paige pulled her hand out from under Austin's. "That was Sabrina," she said coolly. "You told Caleb who you were taking to dinner, didn't you?"

Austin shook his head. "He didn't ask, and I didn't volunteer."

She eyed him warily, but on second thought she realized that he had to be telling the truth. If Caleb had known, Sabrina would have gotten the information out of him, no question about it—and in that case she wouldn't have been stunned at the sight of her partner.

Now that the initial shock was passing, Paige had no trouble guessing what had happened. Caleb had casually mentioned doing Austin a favor by making a dinner reservation for two. Sabrina, itching with curiosity about who Austin might be dating, had suggested they, too, go out for the evening, and then she'd made it a point to casually pass by the one spot in the entire restaurant where it was possible to see down on that particular table—Caleb's favorite table...

Sabrina called, Eileen had told her as Austin arrived. *She said she just wanted to gossip.*

About Austin's date, no doubt. It was a good thing, Paige thought, that she hadn't answered the phone herself—though it would certainly have been an interesting conversation.

"This was a mistake." She pushed back her chair. "I'm leaving."

Austin's eyebrows rose. "Right now? Just as the waiter is bringing our appetizer? All you'll manage to accomplish is to confirm Sabrina's suspicions that there's something really odd going on."

Paige sank back into her chair. He was right, of course; she had to finish out the evening or raise far more questions than she was prepared to answer.

Besides, she thought rebelliously, why shouldn't she have dinner with Austin, anyway? She'd done him a big favor; he was giving her a treat in return. Surely anybody could understand that. And she didn't have to account to her partners for anything she did.

The waiter placed a chilled plate before her. Paige looked at the dainty, perfectly molded salmon mousse with sudden loathing.

"Why is it so important to you what Sabrina thinks, anyway?" Austin asked lazily.

Paige looked straight at him. "Because I don't want her to worry about me. She's afraid, you see, that I'll take you seriously."

"But I am serious, Paige." Austin reached for the wine bottle and topped off her glass. "I meant what I said, before Sabrina popped her head into the conversation."

Paige shook her head. "Sorry. Whatever you were saying, it's gone completely out of my mind."

Austin's jaw tightened for an instant, but his voice was perfectly even, almost casual. "I would like to make your life easier, Paige."

"That's very sweet of you." She said it in the same earnest tone of voice she would have used to thank Jennifer for offering to share a used wad of chewing gum. "But if you're talking again about offering me money—"

Austin shook his head. "Oh, no. I'm asking you to marry me."

CHAPTER NINE

PAIGE felt as if the restaurant had suddenly turned into a carnival ride; the floor not only tipped from side to side but it went up and down, and the table revolved like a merry-go-round. She had to keep her eyes closed for a full minute before things began to stay in their proper places once more.

When she finally found her voice, it was faint and almost squeaky. "Would you mind running that past me again, Austin?"

"You heard me, Paige. I asked if you'll marry me."

He sounded almost impatient, she thought, as if her reaction was throwing off his schedule. As if he'd set aside just enough time for question and answer, with nothing left over for discussion.

Paige sipped her wine. "I don't suppose you'd like to explain why on earth you think it would be a good idea."

Austin frowned. "I thought it would be obvious."

"Maybe you could hit the high spots," she suggested hopefully. "Just so we're both clear on what kind of a deal we're talking about. I mean, you wouldn't want me to get the crazy idea that you've fallen madly in love with me within the last few days. Would you?"

"That would be a little uncomfortable," Austin agreed, "since I haven't done anything of the sort."

"That's what I thought. So why do you want to—" She hoped he'd miss the tiny quaver in her voice. "—marry me?"

He raised one hand to his collar as if it suddenly felt

143

too tight, then seemed to catch himself and fiddled with his tie instead.

Interesting body language, Paige thought, for a guy who every day played corporate poker with millions on the table. A guy who seemed to think he was negotiating just another business deal.

"All the usual reasons," Austin said. "In my position there are times that being married—"

"You've done just fine as a single man up till now."

"Tanner Electronics is different from anywhere else I've ever worked."

"That's true," Paige said judiciously. "There is no doubt whatsoever that all the bimbos whose hearts will be shattered when Caleb finally says 'I do' will soon be looking for other game, and their collective eye will certainly light on you. In fact, since you're something of a mystery man, they might find you even more intriguing."

"Paige, if I wanted a bodyguard I'd hire one."

"Exactly," she murmured. She felt almost as if she was an onlooker, disconnected from her body and watching from a distance, through a sort of numbing haze.

"What I mean is, this job is different. Every other position I've held has been a stepping stone, a rung on the ladder."

"And the job at Tanner is the top of the heap? Caleb will be tickled pink to hear your opinion of his company."

His mouth tightened. "I didn't say that, exactly. But my attitude toward work has changed. I stepped back and took a good look at my life, and I came to the conclusion that there are other ways to better myself than to keep climbing the corporate mountain. I don't want to keep on moving every year or two, and starting all over. Now that Jennifer's in school—"

"I wondered," Paige murmured, "when we'd get to Jennifer."

Austin didn't seem to hear. "I want her to be able to put down roots, to make friends she'll keep forever, to live in a house she'll always remember."

"Don't forget the cat," Paige recommended.

"And take in stray cats, if she feels like it. I intend to stay in Denver, Paige. I want to build a life here."

"So of course a wife would be a handy accessory, in both the business and the personal arenas. I understand all that, Austin. But in fact, I didn't ask why you wanted to get married. I asked why your fancy landed on *me*."

For a long moment she thought he wasn't going to answer. Then he sighed. "All right, if you insist. It's a matter of fairness, as much as anything. We talked about it a few days ago, you know—how deeply indebted I am to you. Your hard work and sacrifice during the time we were married is a significant part of the reason that I'm where I am, and it's not very fair that you shouldn't benefit from my success. So of course when I started considering marriage, I thought of you."

Paige wondered half hysterically if he had any idea of how pompous he sounded. All this talk of fairness and indebtedness—but not a hint of caring, much less of love.

Not that she'd expected it. In fact, she admitted, if he had said anything of the sort she wouldn't have believed it. But he could have gone through the motions. He could at least have tried to scrape up some fondness, some affectionate memories...*something* which would serve as a foundation for another try at marriage. Anything besides a debt.

"So because a few days ago I wouldn't let you give me money," she mused, "you're now proposing marriage. That doesn't make a great deal of sense."

"It wasn't cause-and-effect, Paige, but that discussion started me thinking about you. About doing what's right. You're struggling financially, that's obvious." He reached across the table once more.

Paige moved her hand out of range. How dare he patronize her? *Doing what's right*...as if she was no more than a child who needed to be looked after and provided for! "I'm so glad you mentioned that," she said grimly, "because I hadn't happened to notice it myself. I think I'm doing just fine."

"Not compared to what I can offer you. What if the roof needs replacing? What if your van breaks down and you have to buy a new one?"

"It's so generous of you to have only my best interests at heart," Paige murmured. "Obviously you've considered my house and my van. What about my mother? I'm sure you've taken her into account and decided what to do with her."

"If you don't think she's able to take care of herself, we'll look for a house with a self-contained suite."

"You'd actually share a roof with the dragon on wheels? You have come a long way, haven't you, Austin?" Her tone was almost admiring. "Or are you so certain she'd refuse that you feel safe in making the offer?" She didn't give him a chance to respond, but there was no mistaking the fact that he'd turned ever-so-slightly red.

She twirled her wineglass and said thoughtfully, "Of course, this proposal doesn't have anything to do with the nanny shortage." She stole a look at him through lowered eyelashes. "Does it?"

"There isn't any lack of nannies," Austin said flatly. "I'm not proposing to you because I want a live-in baby-sitter."

She clasped her hands over her heart in a theatrical gesture. "No? What an honor you've paid me! To know that you prefer me to ordinary hired help—"

"Dammit, Paige, this has nothing to do with nannies! All right, so Jennifer likes you. I should think that would be anything but a deterrent."

"In fact, a ready-made family should be a great enticement, is that what you're saying?" She sighed. "Look, Austin, I'm very flattered." Even though she tried, she couldn't keep the edge of sarcasm out of her voice. "In fact, you cannot possibly understand the depth of my emotions on this occasion. So let's just say—"

"Wait a minute, Paige. Before you throw this opportunity away, at least stop to consider what you're giving up. Security, for one. Your business is going to go down the drain, and—"

The absolute certainty in his voice terrified Paige. "Are you threatening Rent-A-Wife?" she demanded.

"Marry me or I'll ruin your business? I don't have either time or inclination for such childish nonsense. It's a simple fact, and you'd know it, too, if you stopped long enough to take an honest look at your business."

"On what evidence are you basing that grandstand statement?"

"Sabrina and Cassie have other priorities now. They're already working fewer hours. So far, you've been taking up the slack, but you're not going to be able to keep up alone. Clients will be unhappy at not getting what they need when they want it. You'll be stressed past your limits." He shrugged. "It's obvious."

As a matter of fact, he was right. Paige had seen that very trend herself—it was why she'd started to take seriously the idea of bringing in another partner—but she was damned if she'd admit it to Austin. "Oh, if *that's* all... I came up with the idea originally, and I ran the business by myself for a few months before the others joined. I can do it again. I'll pare the client list—''

"And work yourself to the bone and barely make ends meet. All that isn't necessary, Paige. There's an alternative to running Rent-A-Wife.''

"Yeah. All I have to do is let you rent me full-time.''

He gritted his teeth; she actually heard them grind. "That's not the kind of arrangement I'm suggesting, Paige.''

"How silly of me,'' she said on a note of discovery. "You mean I'd have additional duties. Bed-warmer, for starters.''

"There's no need to be crude.''

"I'm not, just factual. I don't think you can tell me with a straight face that you're proposing some kind of platonic relationship. Are you?''

"No,'' he said slowly.

"Then 'bed-warmer' is part of the job description.''

His voice was as rich as warm fudge. "Would it be such a horrible thing, Paige? You can't deny you always enjoyed yourself in our bed.''

She didn't know if the shivers which ran up her spine were delicious memories of how very much she'd enjoyed herself, or distaste at the idea of sleeping with a man who considered her nothing more than a convenience. "That,'' she said crisply, "was when I thought I loved you.''

"*Love.*'' He dismissed it with a gesture. "We were foolish enough to think all that nonsense would last forever. It didn't—and so what? You can't deny there's still an attraction. If there wasn't, you wouldn't look terrified every time I come near you. You're the one who mentioned making an alliance—''

"Oh, no,'' Paige said hastily. "Don't even try to blame

this crazy idea on me. The answer is no. Absolutely, un-equivocally no. And I don't want to hear another word on the subject.''

She picked up her fork and jabbed it into the salmon mousse. Too bad, she thought, that it wasn't Austin's heart lying on her plate, because she'd positively enjoy carving it to ribbons. Of course, that was assuming he *had* a heart, and she wouldn't bet any money on the possibility.

He'd certainly blown that one, Austin told himself gloomily.

But what other approach could he have taken? He'd been convinced Paige was the kind of woman who wouldn't duck from reality. The sort who would appreciate honesty.

Apparently he'd been wrong.

But even to feed her ego, he couldn't have forced himself to drop to one knee and make protestations of a love that didn't in fact exist. He wasn't a hypocrite, and it wouldn't have been respectful to act out what he didn't feel. Surely she understood that much.

Love…what the hell was it, anyway?

Now if they'd been discussing desire, he reflected, that would have been another thing entirely. He could have gone into vivid detail about how much he wanted to make love to her. He could have painted a couple of dozen erotic scenarios without even beginning to stretch the truth.…

That was odd. He hadn't realized till just this moment that every aspect of those scenes was already quite clear in his mind. Since when had he been fantasizing about Paige McDermott?

Though, on further consideration, he didn't know why he should be surprised. Once, he had known her body as intimately as his own. A man didn't forget things like that,

even if he tucked the knowledge into the farthest, darkest
corner of his mind for a while. As soon as she'd come
back into his life, though, the memories had crept out of
hiding. They'd oozed around the protective wall he'd built
to confine them, and squirmed like tentacles into his un-
guarded thoughts, building themselves into fantasies...

Memories of Paige...who could be innocent and erotic,
naive and seductive—sometimes all at the same moment.

Paige...who had looked at him as though he'd lost his
mind, simply because he'd proposed to her.

What was the matter with the woman, anyway?

When their main course arrived, Paige pushed bits of her
filet mignon around her plate, making trails in the béar-
naise sauce, till the meat was cold and the sauce congealed.
The conversation limped from one unimportant topic to
the next, and she was relieved when finally the waiter
cleared the table and asked if they'd like coffee and a look
at the dessert tray.

Paige was just opening her mouth to say a firm no when
Austin pushed back his chair and stood up. Silent though
it was, the action made his opinion pretty clear, she
thought. In rude but definite terms, he was announcing that
dinner was over.

Paige gave the waiter an apologetic little smile.
Actually, she couldn't quite decide whether to be annoyed
that Austin was so obviously afraid she wanted to prolong
the evening, or irritated that he'd been rude to the waiter,
or pleased that at last she could escape...

Then she glanced over her shoulder to see what Austin
was looking at and realized that she'd missed the mark on
all counts. He hadn't been responding to the waiter's question at all; he'd stood up to greet the two people who were

approaching the table from the main section of the restaurant, directly behind Paige.

"Sabrina," he said. "Caleb. It's a pleasure."

For a split second, Paige considered reaching for the flickering candle at the center of the table and setting her own dress on fire. Self-immolation seemed a small price to pay for having the paramedics rescue her. But sanity quickly returned. She'd only end up in a hospital bed where she would stand no chance of dodging Sabrina's questions. And at least with Austin standing right there, Sabrina would have to control her curiosity.

"I'd invite you to join us for dessert," Austin was saying, "except—"

"Except for the inconvenient fact that it's a table for two," Sabrina murmured, "which is precisely why it's always been Caleb's favorite. In any case, we came to invite *you* to join *us* for dessert."

Paige bit her tongue just in time to stop herself from saying that she really didn't want to do anything of the sort and forced a smile instead. Austin flicked a glance at her and then agreed, sounding perfectly calm, that dessert would be very nice indeed.

"Come along then," Sabrina said, and linked her arm in Paige's.

Paige tossed a pleading glance over her shoulder, but Austin had turned away to deal with the bill.

Sabrina didn't stop till they reached the cloakroom in the elevator lobby.

"I thought you said something about dessert," Paige protested. "Or was that just a tactful way to get us away from the table? I've got it, the tower's on fire and only a few people can be saved, so you wanted to remove us from the room to be rescued without causing panic among the ones who'll be left behind."

"Not a bad plot twist," Sabrina said. "But you can stop babbling anytime. And as for dessert, you know perfectly well you don't care about it anymore than I do."

"Well, no," Paige admitted. "But—"

"So what the *hell* are you doing with Austin Weaver?"

Caleb spoke from just behind Sabrina. "Having dinner, darling. The rest is none of your business."

Paige had always liked the playboy entrepreneur, even when she'd thought he was an irresponsible scamp who was toying with Sabrina's heart because he had nothing better to do. But she'd never liked him quite so well as she did right then.

Caleb grinned at her. "Anyway, we're taking one of Pierre's cakes home with us."

"It's not a cake, Caleb, it's a white chocolate and raspberry torte." Sabrina handed over a ticket and reclaimed a fur- trimmed wrap. "Aren't you going to get your coat, Paige?"

"Home?" Paige said faintly. Caleb's rescue attempt had been short-lived. So much for her hopes of making a quick escape before Sabrina could get her in a choke hold.

Sabrina's voice was airy. "Oh, didn't I mention that?" She turned to Austin, who had just come up to them, one hand still sliding a slim wallet into his breast pocket. "You don't need directions to the house, do you? It's a different route than you've come before, so if you'd like to just follow us—"

The parking valets brought Austin's Jaguar and Sabrina's vintage convertible to the front of the building; Sabrina dangled her keys invitingly and said, "Want to ride with me, Paige, so the men can talk shop? They will, anyway, but maybe if we put them in the same car, they'll get it over with sooner."

"I—" Paige caught at the first excuse she could think

of. "It'll be hard to keep two cars together, in this traffic. I'd better ride with Austin so I can point out the turns."

"I think Caleb could manage to find his way home," Sabrina said dryly. But she didn't push the matter, and a moment later the little convertible sped off into the night.

Paige sank as far as possible into the passenger seat of the Jaguar and rubbed her aching temples. "Did you have to accept the invitation?"

"Surely you're not seriously suggesting there was an alternative. Besides, you seemed to approve—smiling like that."

She sat up. "What was I supposed to do? Send you a telegram?"

"I suppose I could have told them we were having a very serious conversation about marriage—"

"We were not."

"Are you saying it wasn't serious or that it wasn't about marriage? Because I assure you—"

"We weren't talking at all," Paige pointed out. "Which, come to think of it, isn't a bad idea." She turned her back to him and stared unseeing out the window. Blocks went by in a blur.

"Look," Austin said, "I'm sorry. Obviously I didn't handle that discussion very well."

Paige looked over her shoulder. "Noticed that, did you?" she asked admiringly. "I bet you'd figure it out right away if an elephant landed in your eye, too!"

"There isn't any need to be sarcastic about it." His voice was so quiet she had to strain to hear him.

Paige bit her lip. She felt like a scolded child, even though it had been a gentler reproof than she deserved. "No," she said quietly. "There isn't. You made an offer, I refused it, and that's the end of it."

It had been the only possible end. She had given the

only possible answer. So there was no reason, Paige told herself, for the sneaking suspicion that it wasn't over, after all.

Much to Paige's surprise, they were not the only guests at the dessert party. Cassie and Jake Abbott were already there when Austin and Paige arrived, drinking brandy and coffee in Caleb's newly redecorated living room.

Paige's first reaction was relief, for Cassie was normally the voice of reason which served as a balance for Sabrina's sometimes-overwhelming zeal. Then she saw the narrowed look Cassie threw at her when she came in with Austin. She remembered the conversation they'd had over lunch just a couple of days ago and wondered if she was in for a reenactment of the Spanish Inquisition.

The worst of it, she thought, was that her partners' concern sprang not from nosiness or a desire to control, but from love. Cassie and Sabrina honestly cared. They were truly worried about her.

She deliberately chose a seat next to Cassie and just as purposefully started a conversation she liked better than the topic she suspected her partner had in mind. "How did Ben Orcutt's party go?"

Cassie shook her head. "He hasn't held it yet. I told him he'd better give me at least a couple of days notice or he'll get Chinese take-out instead of real cuisine."

"If Sabrina's right in thinking he's in love, he won't even notice."

"I couldn't be that lucky," Cassie said.

Caleb's butler provided Paige and Austin with coffee and brandy, and vanished to answer the door once more. Sabrina struck a pose in the center of the room. "No doubt you're all wondering why we've gathered you together tonight."

Paige sipped her coffee and watched as another couple came into the living room. *That'll teach you to be egotistical,* she told herself. Whatever was going on tonight, it couldn't be aimed at Paige, for the newest arrivals were Caleb's parents.

Their presence kicked off a totally different kind of suspicion in Paige's mind. *Surely not,* she thought. *Sabrina wouldn't.*

"It's because of my mother, actually," Sabrina went on.

Cassie sounded resigned. "What's she done this time?"

"As if adding two extra bridesmaids and inviting a couple of hundred additional guests wasn't enough," Sabrina said, "she's now decided that the reception we've planned isn't at all the kind of thing her friends will expect. She feels there needs to be another band and that the menu isn't quite as refined as it should be.... Well, anyway, I'm sure you get the picture."

"The picture's perfectly clear," Jake said. "I just don't see what it has to do with dessert. You promised me white chocolate and raspberries."

Sabrina gave him a blinding smile. "Don't worry, we really did bring a torte home, but you'll have to wait just a little while for it. Caleb and I have decided that since my mother is so determined to make this wedding her party instead of ours, we're going to let her have it all to herself. We'll show up at her party for the sake of being polite to all of the guests—but we're getting married now instead of in that circus."

"Now?" Paige asked. "You mean—right now?"

Sabrina nodded. "It was your idea that we elope, you know."

"I was just remembering that," Paige said wryly.

"But we decided we couldn't possibly get married without the people who are most important to us. That's why we sort of inveigled and manipulated and practically kidnapped to get you all here—for the wedding.'' She looked straight at Paige. "You were the real problem. I've spent most of the evening trying to find you, because when I called back your mother would only say that you were out. You could have knocked me over when I went after Austin and got you, too.''

"Glad to oblige," Austin said under his breath. "Anything to help out a friend."

Caleb slapped him on the back and raised his voice. "Your Honor, I think we're ready."

From the sunroom came a silver-haired man, book in hand, and stood in front of the fireplace. "If you'll gather around me in a semicircle, please…"

Paige put down her coffee cup and went to stand beside Cassie. From her position at the end of the curve, she could see everyone else without even turning her head. Cassie, still looking stunned. Sabrina and Caleb, with eyes only for each other. Caleb's parents, as calm as if they did this every day. Jake, obviously resigned to waiting for dessert. And Austin…

She didn't want to think about Austin in any context involving weddings, so she turned her mind instead to the contrasts between the ceremony Sabrina had planned and the one which was actually happening. No stately organ marches, just the whisper of background music from the CD system. No enormous baskets of exotic flowers, just a vase on the mantel containing half a dozen roses. No fancy dresses…

Her own Edwardian costume, Paige thought, must still be hanging upstairs in the guest room where she'd tried it on, the day Austin came to town. It would probably never be worn, now. But that was nothing next to the waste of Sabrina's gorgeous white satin and lace gown.

It was obvious, however, that none of those things mattered to the couple standing in front of the fireplace. The only thing that counted was the love which shone in their eyes as they promised their lives to each other.

Once, Paige thought, she had felt like that.

How bitterly ironic it was, she mused, that this simple, beautiful ceremony had followed so closely on the heels of Austin's chilly proposal. She wondered if he was capable of recognizing the contrast.

She glanced across the circle at him, and realized too late that he was watching her. His dark, straightforward gaze captured hers and held her fast, and her heartbeat speeded up.

Once they, too, had stood together in front of a judge, and pledged their love and their lives to each other....

The judge's words were little more than an irritating murmur in the back of Paige's mind, for as she looked across the room at Austin the pieces fell into place, and she understood why his proposal had so infuriated her, and why she had slashed back at him with sarcasm.

She hadn't been insulted, she'd been hurt. Grievously wounded, in fact, that by reducing his proposal to a cold-hearted bargain he had as much as said that their marriage had meant nothing to him. That the love she continued to feel was as insignificant as ever...

Wait a minute, she told herself. *I don't still love him. I can't still love him!*

Panic made her breathless. Yes, she had loved him once. She had sworn to love and honor and cherish him for the rest of their lives. But that had all been over the day he walked out on her. He hadn't kept his promises, and therefore she was released from hers. That was the moment she had closed the door on loving him—

Something seemed to tear loose deep inside her. No, she

admitted, that wasn't quite the truth. She hadn't closed the door on loving him, she'd simply stopped allowing herself to feel anything at all. She hadn't gotten over Austin, she'd denied that there was anything to get over.

Through the years since, she'd convinced herself that she had healed, and that her lack of interest in men and romance was because she had more important matters to tend to. In fact, it was because Austin still held her heart.

She had made her vows in faith and in love. And she had continued to keep them, all the while denying it even to herself. That was because of pride, she supposed—it was only human not to want to admit that she could still care so deeply for someone who had rejected her.

Someone who now wanted to marry her again...for all the wrong reasons.

They could hardly walk out straight after the ceremony, with an impromptu reception under way. Besides, as long as Paige stayed on the opposite side of the room from Austin she almost enjoyed herself—and in any case she wasn't eager to be alone with him, even for the short while it would take for him to drive her home. At least not until she'd had a little time to absorb the shock of her new knowledge, to come to terms with the discovery that she still cared about him, to decide what she was going to do.

Not that it made an ounce of difference in how she had answered his question. If anything, the revelation strengthened her conviction that she'd done the right thing in refusing him. It would be bad enough to enter into a marriage with no love on either side; it would be virtual suicide to deliberately marry a man she loved, knowing that he did not care about her.

But eventually he cornered her in the kitchen, where

she'd carried a stack of dessert plates. "Isn't that the butler's job, Paige?"

"It wouldn't be the first time I've helped Jennings clean up this kitchen. In fact," she said thoughtfully, "I've probably spent more time in this room than Sabrina has."

"Nevertheless, it's time to go. The starry-eyed bride and the shell-shocked groom would no doubt like to be alone."

And sometime I have to face you again, she thought. *I suppose we might as well get it over with.*

"Shell-shocked?" she asked as the Jaguar pulled onto the street. "What did you mean by that?"

"Just that Caleb looked as if he couldn't believe he'd actually said the words."

"Is that any surprise? He's been known as the playboy entrepreneur for years." She added, almost under her breath, "But maybe that wasn't the reason at all. Maybe he looked that way because he couldn't believe he's actually got Sabrina for his very own."

Austin didn't take his eyes off the oncoming cars as he waited to make a turn. "What did you say?"

"Nothing that mattered." *Nothing that you'd understand.* "I didn't realize how late it was."

"Will your mother be worried about you?"

Anyone else would have thought the question was perfectly straightforward, but Paige heard the ironic edge in Austin's voice. "She's concerned when I'm out at night," she said levelly. "So were you a few days ago, as I recall."

He shot a look at her. "Eileen is nowhere near as old as she looks—and acts."

"What's that supposed to mean?"

"That she doesn't need you nearly as much as you think she does. So if you turned me down because of her—"

"I didn't. And I hardly think you're the best judge of how much my mother needs me."

"I'm not asking you to turn your back on her, you know. I just believe she's much more capable of looking after herself than you think."

"Oh? What happened to the idea of buying a house with a suite for her?"

"If that's what you want—"

"It isn't. You're off the hook, Austin."

As soon as the Jaguar stopped in the bungalow's driveway, Paige had the door open. "Thank you for dinner," she said without looking at him. "It's been a very interesting evening."

He turned off the engine and came around the car.

It would be undignified, Paige told herself, to scurry toward the house like a frightened rabbit. So he intended to walk her to the door; what was the big deal about that? He certainly wasn't planning to ravish her on the front porch!

She fumbled for her key and cursed herself for not having it out and ready. Did he have to stand so close to her? Her fingers were trembling.

"You have to look at me sometime, Paige. You might as well not try to hide."

Paige concentrated on her key as if it were the most fascinating thing in the universe. She could feel the warmth of him as he moved even closer.

"You know perfectly well what would happen," he said very softly, "if you went to bed with me tonight. I haven't forgotten how to make you scream with pleasure—"

Be casual, she told herself. *You mustn't let him think it matters, whatever he says.*

"Now that's a good reason *not* to go to bed with you,"

she murmured. "In this part of town, if the neighbors hear screams they call the cops."

His warm chuckle startled her, and before Paige could stop herself she shot a look up at him.

Suddenly his lips came down on hers, not fiercely but with a sureness which terrified her more than violence could, because he was so obviously certain that he could arouse her, and because he was so obviously right. She had tried to forget that particular kiss—the soft, sensual, teasing one which could disarm her ire, interrupt her concentration, distract her from any task, melt her bones...but the memory of it was written in her cells, and her traitorous body responded exactly as it always had.

The only difference was that in the seven years since he'd last used it on her, Austin had gotten nothing but better.

Her open palm cracked against his cheek, but he didn't let her go immediately. He held her shoulders and forced her to look at him. "It's not over, Paige." His voice was raw.

She could manage little more than a whisper. "Yes, it is."

He walked away, and she let herself into the house and leaned against the front door.

It *was* all over, she told herself, and the only thing left to do was to heal her wounds. If she was lucky, it might only take a couple of centuries.

CHAPTER TEN

AUSTIN heard the lock of the front door click behind him as he retreated to his car. He could see his breath, rapid puffs against the frigid air. The inside of the Jaguar smelled like vanilla. He wondered if her perfume was in the air, or if she'd branded it on his skin.

"Idiot," he muttered. Losing control of himself like that simply because Paige had cast a shy and—he would have sworn—inviting look up at him!

A gentleman would have let go of her at the first hint of protest, taken a large step backward, and apologized for acting like a Neanderthal.

All right, he admitted, so he wasn't a gentleman. He hadn't taken her at her word and retired from the battle-field, he'd issued a challenge instead. *It's not over, Paige...*

And dammit, he told himself, it *wasn't* over—because, in the instant before she'd taken that swing at him, she'd kissed him back. She had gone lax in his arms and her lips had softened under his. Despite the weight of her winter coat, her body had molded itself to his.

Her surrender had lasted only a matter of seconds, and he was certain she'd deny it had ever happened. But he knew the truth. Those few fleeting moments had been plenty long enough for him to taste capitulation and to savor triumph. For a few seconds, he had felt absolutely drunk with success.

And then she'd slapped him. Of course, that was no wonder. The way he'd grabbed her, held her, kissed her—

162

what in hell was wrong with him, anyway? To so carelessly throw away the ground he'd gained—

What ground? he asked himself cynically. *Don't kid
yourself, Weaver. You hadn't gotten anywhere all evening—and that's why you grabbed her like some oversexed
teenager.*

He'd dealt himself a setback, that was apparent—and
obviously he needed a new and different approach.

But giving up wasn't an option. Not when she'd kissed
him like that.

It felt like eons, but Paige had probably been standing by
the front door for only a couple of minutes when Eileen
coughed.

It took her a moment, though, to realize that the sound
hadn't come from her mother's bedroom down the hall,
but from just across the room. Wearily, she opened her
eyes.

All the lights were off, but by the dim glow of the street
lamps Paige saw Eileen's chair drawn up in her favorite
spot.

"I'd ask if you had a pleasant evening," Eileen said,
"but the answer is apparent." She started to cough again,
a dry hack that seemed to tear at her chest.

Automatically, Paige crossed the room and laid the back
of her hand against Eileen's forehead. It felt hot and dry,
and the sensation was just as familiar as the cough was. It
might not be pneumonia again, but there was no time to
lose in getting it checked out.

"I suspected you were feverish earlier," Paige muttered.
"But then I got distracted. I'll warm up the van and take
you to the hospital."

When she came back a few minutes later, carrying

Eileen's winter coat, she was frowning. "Why is Jennifer's cat shut up on the back porch?"

"Because it's cold outside."

"So you brought that animal into the house? Fleas and all?"

"I figured any fleas on her would have frozen to death by now." Eileen had to stop to catch her breath. "Besides, she's only on the porch, and that's just till you can take her to the vet to have her checked out."

"She'll probably claw her way out through a window."

Eileen shook her head. "I don't think so. She's not really wild, you know, she's just starved. And someone has been mean to her."

"Do I want to know how you managed to lure her inside, when the rest of us can barely get near her?" Except for Austin, Paige thought. The cat had taken to him almost instantaneously. *Some females are like that*, she thought.

"I sat on the back porch with the door propped open and talked to her till she came to me."

Paige stared at her mother. "No wonder you've got a cough—you deserve double pneumonia! Why in the name of heaven—" She stopped as Eileen went off into another coughing spasm. "You miss her, don't you? Jennifer, I mean."

When Eileen regained her breath, she said, with a trace of acid in her voice, "I'm not a fool, Paige. I may not exactly like the way things are shaping up, but I can't help but see the pattern."

"What pattern?" Paige asked irritably.

"Austin inviting you out. The way you look at him."

And what way do I supposedly look at him? Paige knew better than to ask; she was afraid to find out what her mother might have noticed. Though surely, when she herself hadn't understood that she still loved him, no one else could have guessed it. Could they?

"You could do worse, I suppose," Eileen mused.

If Paige's nerves hadn't still been raw from Austin's cool and businesslike proposal, she probably would have ignored the comment. Instead, she snapped, "Better the devil I know—is that what you're saying? Forget it, Mother. You're seeing things that aren't there."

Eileen looked at her through narrowed eyes. "You've missed a lot, Paige." Her voice was almost gentle. "I didn't realize how much until I saw you with Jennifer." Then she started coughing again.

By morning, Austin had regained his balance and even his sense of humor. As he drank his coffee and tried in vain to hurry Jennifer through her breakfast so she wouldn't be late for school, he stood looking out at the crisp and chilly day and reconsidering the events of the evening before.

Well, fine, he told himself. If Paige wanted him to leave her alone, that was how it would be. He could take a hint. And it wasn't as if he was desperate for her attention, anyway.

He'd simply had a good idea, that was all. A plan which would have benefited them both. But if she didn't see it that way, it was her privilege to turn down the offer.

"If you're finished," he told Jennifer, "put your plate in the dishwasher and get your coat on."

Anyway, it wasn't as if there weren't other women, he thought. And though it sounded a little vain even to think about it, the fact was that plenty of those women would appreciate the very package that Paige had so contemptuously turned down.

"Don't forget your backpack, Jen," he added automatically.

Not every woman in the world would find what he had to offer overwhelmingly attractive, of course; he wasn't arrogant enough to think that. But he wasn't exactly hard on the eyes. He was a good provider. His daughter was well-behaved and even charming.

Yes, he'd have a choice.

He'd felt it was only right to make the offer to Paige first, that was all. But now that she'd turned him down, he'd simply start looking around. And when Paige realized what he was doing—

He pulled himself up short. Changing Paige's mind, he told himself, was not the goal.

In the lobby, Jennifer balked. "I'm cold," she complained.

"I didn't notice the weather bothering you when you were playing in the snow at Paige's house."

Her big brown eyes were accusing. "Things were different at Paige's. There's no snow I can play in here, and I can't even have my cat."

He squatted to her level and tied the hood of her coat. "Maybe we can fix a couple of those things. If we went to live in a house—"

Behind him, Tricia Cade said, "A house? Do you mean you're unhappy here, Austin?"

He smothered a sigh. Had the woman been lurking in the hallway, waiting for them to come down?

He ought to have known better than to take her to Sabrina's party. Now every time he turned around, Tricia Cade was lying in wait for him. He supposed it was no more than he deserved.

He stood up. "Aspen Towers is great, Tricia. But you heard Jennifer—no snow to play in, no cats allowed."

"Also no lawn to take care of, no roof to fix, no leaves to rake…"

He shrugged. "Those things might be kind of fun."

Tricia gave a patronizing laugh which didn't go well with her sultry tone. "I see I'll have to do some work to convince you that this is where you want to be."

He saw Jennifer roll her eyes, and he seized her by the top of her hood and hauled her out to the car before she could start making gagging noises.

"What kind of a house?" Jennifer asked.

"I don't know. We'll have to see what's for sale."

"I like Paige's house."

"Paige's house is not one of the choices." He said it as pleasantly as he could, but his voice was firm nevertheless. There would be no kindness to the child in allowing her to cherish impossible illusions.

Jennifer settled into her seat and stuck her lower lip out.

Austin recognized the pose. His daughter knew quite well that she wasn't going to get what she wanted, and she was too dignified to throw a useless tantrum. She was, however, making sure he realized that his decision had absolutely destroyed any chance of her ever being happy again.

Usually she held out for ten minutes or so, and then she'd get distracted and forget whatever it was that had been so important. This time, he expected, the treatment would last a little longer. But Jennifer would get over it and move on.

Just as he had.

He congratulated himself. He'd made his decision to cut his losses, and he'd started to look around at the alternatives.

Of course, the first candidate who'd appeared fell a great deal short of the requirements. The woman he wanted to marry was nothing like Tricia Cade. He was looking for someone who was gentle, caring, and able to laugh even

at her own expense. Not the clinging vine type. Interested
in people and things, and interesting to be with. She had
to be fond of his daughter, and—of course—of him.

And as long as he was making a list, he thought wryly,
he might as well go all the way; she didn't have to be a
beauty queen, but if she was nicely shaped and sexy as
hell, that wouldn't hurt his feelings, either. In fact, now
that he thought about it, his ideal woman wasn't at all hard
to picture. If he closed his eyes and visualized her...

He saw Paige.

Paige, with the friends who were closer to her than sisters. Paige, bending over Jennifer in the snow. Paige, looking up at him last night, in the instant when he'd thought
he saw desire in her eyes...

You're just ticked off because she turned you down, he
told himself. *Get over it, Weaver.*

But a little voice at the back of his brain whispered, *Do
you really think you can?*

Austin didn't realize till he tried to go through the security
checkpoint in the atrium lobby that he'd left his identification pass at home. He knew exactly where it was. He
could picture it, lying between a pair of onyx cufflinks and
the note, still unsigned, which Jennifer was supposed to
have taken back to the academy today so she could go on
a field trip with her class.

Unfortunately, the security guard was in no mood to
trust Austin's word. He pulled out his driver's license, but
it only served to confuse the issue when the guard wanted
to know why it had been issued in Georgia if Austin really
worked in Colorado. A second guard appeared; Austin
started over.

He was still embroiled in the discussion when Caleb
came through the main door, pulled off his motorcycle

helmet, flashed his pass at the guard, and stopped dead at the sight of his new CEO in the grip of security. "Having a little problem, are we?" he asked genially.

"It would be helpful if you would tell them who I am," Austin said, trying not to grit his teeth.

"You mean vouch for your character? Sure. Hey, guys, let him through. He'll bring in two ID passes tomorrow, just to make you happy."

Austin stepped through the checkpoint.

"I just hope you don't mind if they have two different names on them," Caleb said over his shoulder. He grinned at Austin. "I told you the staff wouldn't like your new security measures. I just didn't expect *you* to be the first one to make a fuss."

"All right," Austin admitted. "Maybe I went a little too far in protecting the place. Is that what you want to hear?"

"No, I'm more interested in why you don't have your pass. Forgetting things is the first symptom, as I recall."

"The first symptom of what?"

"Rent-A-Wife syndrome. Want to stop in the cafeteria and get a doughnut?"

Austin shuddered. "I tried one yesterday, thanks. Paige is right, we have to do something about the cafeteria."

"And that's the second symptom. Bringing her name into the conversation at every opportunity."

Austin decided to ignore the implication. Caleb was only fishing for information, anyway; Sabrina had no doubt put him up to it. "I didn't expect to see you anywhere near this place today."

"My beautiful bride got saddled with answering Rent-A-Wife's phones, so I figured I might as well stay out of her way." Caleb followed Austin into the corner office.

"I thought Paige's mother usually took care of that."

Caleb grinned. "There's that second symptom again. She does, except today Eileen's in the hospital."

Austin was startled. "But— When did that happen?"

"Sometime last night, obviously. Probably about the time Paige got home. Whenever that was."

Austin let the innuendo pass. "Which hospital?" He saw Caleb's eyebrow lift and said irritably, "I thought I'd send flowers."

Caleb unzipped the tight sleeves of his black leather jacket and sat down, propping his boots on the corner of the desk. "I should have warned you as soon as you came on board," he said. "About this Rent-A-Wife business, I mean. At first, it's just a casual thing. Handy. Sensible. But if you aren't careful, the next thing you know you're signing a purchase agreement."

Austin grinned. "It can't be the worst idea of all time. You did it."

"This head over heels business," Caleb mused, "is the most uncomfortable feeling in the world. Sort of like being hungry all the time, but there's only one dish that will satisfy the appetite. But why am I telling you all this? You obviously already know it." He took his feet off the desk, picked up his helmet, and went out. He was whistling.

Only one dish that will satisfy...

It was long past time to admit the truth, Austin told himself. Caleb had rubbed his nose in the facts just now, but he hadn't revealed anything new—just things Austin was already aware of but hadn't wanted to face.

It wasn't just Tricia Cade he'd rejected this morning, when he'd so blithely run down his list of requirements for a wife. It was every woman in the world who wasn't Paige.

And there was nothing new about that fact, either. He hadn't invited Tricia to Sabrina's party because she was

he only woman he'd met in the short time he'd been back
n Denver. He'd invited her because he was well aware
hat Paige didn't like her—and because he'd been piqued
ecause Paige would rather spend the evening with a five-
ear-old than with him.

Even that long ago, he'd been feeling the hunger.

Only one dish that will satisfy... But the woman whose
aste he craved had turned him down flat. Now the ques-
ion was, what was he going to do about it?

When the therapist came to give Eileen a treatment to help
er breathe more easily, Paige paced the halls for a while
nd came back with yet another cup of muddy hospital
offee. She didn't want it, but holding the cup gave her
omething to do.

As she turned the corner nearest Eileen's room, she ran
lmost headlong into Austin. Her heart rocked with sur-
rise and sudden joy, followed with lightning speed by
ain. Why did he have to come here? And why—with her
ecision made—did she still want to stare at him, to absorb
very detail?

Her mother's words echoed through Paige's mind. *The
ay you look at him...*

If Eileen had noticed, then Paige must be additionally
areful around Austin. If he recognized the longing that
ay so deep within her, Paige wasn't sure she could bear
o see pity in his eyes. On the other hand, if he didn't
bserve what she was feeling, it would be because he
adn't bothered to really look at her—and that would al-
nost be worse yet.

"How's your mother doing?" he asked.

"She'll probably be home tomorrow. We caught it in
ime, before it developed into pneumonia." She turned to-
vard the child standing beside him. Jennifer was holding

an enormous, dense fern, the pot hugged to her chest wit
both arms and the foliage almost hiding her face. "I'v
never seen a plant with legs before, Austin," Paige muse
"What kind of a florist sold you that?"

Jennifer giggled. "It's me, silly."

Paige made a show of parting the foliage to make sur
the child was really there. "Well, come in and set it dow
Eileen's pretty tired, though."

Jennifer nodded earnestly. "Daddy told me she woul
be." She slid sideways through the half-open door. "H
Eileen. I brought you a plant. I picked it out myself."

Eileen's voice was softer than Paige had ever heard i
"It's beautiful, dear. Put it down and come sit with me—
and wait till you hear about your cat."

As Paige started into the room, Austin stepped into he
path. "Wait just a minute. Please. I know you said yo
didn't want to hear another word, but I can't let it res
there. I realize this isn't the time or the place—"

"You're right about that much," Paige said dryly. Be
hind her, a man cleared his throat. Another therapist, sh
thought. "We're blocking the door, Austin."

The man said, sounding very cautious, "Is this Mr
McDermott's room?"

She recognized the voice—but this was the last plac
she'd have expected to hear it. What was Ben Orcutt doin
standing outside Eileen's hospital room?

She turned, and her eyes widened at the sight of Be
wearing the loudest combination of suit, shirt, and tie she'
ever seen, clutching a handful of flowers. She nodde
speech was beyond her.

Ben thanked her politely and went in.

"I didn't know Eileen had an admirer," Austin said.

"Neither did I. Those flowers you didn't send—I won

...er..." That had been the day after the dishwashing lesson, she recalled.

From beyond the door, Jennifer said cheerfully, "Hello, Mr. Orcutt."

Austin's eyebrows rose. "That was Ben Orcutt?"

"Eileen, my dear," Ben said. "When I called you to arrange a time for our special dinner, someone else answered and told me you were here. What happened?"

Paige wondered if she was possibly hearing right. *Our special dinner?* "If he has the nerve to use the gift certificate I gave him to throw a dinner party for *my mother*—"

"Any reason he shouldn't?" Austin asked. "If it was a gift, he can use it any way he likes. Or are you really saying he shouldn't be hanging around Eileen at all? Because if that's what you're thinking, Paige, you need to step back and take a good look at yourself."

She glared at him. "If you're implying that I want her to be dependent on me for some sick reason of my own—"

"No. I think you're just shocked to find that there's more to the old girl than you realized." Austin's voice softened. "I was wrong last night, Paige. Your mother does need you—at least sometimes. But I'm not asking you to leave her. You don't have to choose."

Paige shook her head. "There isn't any choice to make."

"Isn't there?" He moved a little closer. "Please give me another chance, Paige. I said it all wrong last night, and—"

A nurse came down the corridor to Eileen's room, and they stepped aside to let her through.

"If we could go someplace quiet," Austin said wryly, "and just talk... I don't mean right now, of course, but when your mother's better. Just please don't shut me out in the meantime, Paige. Give me a chance—"

"How flattering." Her throat felt tight. "You sound quite desperate—as if you need me."

His hands clamped on her shoulders. "I *do* need you. You have no idea—"

She looked him straight in the eye. "No, Austin. You don't need anyone. Not anyone human, anyway. What you need is a robot—a nicely programmed robot with interchangeable circuit boards."

She shrugged out of his grasp and turned toward Eileen's room. Then, as if it were an afterthought, she looked back at him. "Maybe that's Tanner's next big project," she said. "The one that will really make millions. There must be lots of guys like you who don't know the difference between one woman and another. Certainly enough to make the project a smashing success!"

It was a great exit line. She only wished she could stop trembling long enough to enjoy her triumph.

When it came to party planning, Paige thought, the last minute details were always the worst. Inevitably, something went wrong. The caterer messed up, or the decorations sagged, or the rented furniture didn't arrive on time, or the linens didn't fit.

Or, she thought with foreboding when she caught a glimpse of Austin crossing the atrium toward her, the host decided at the last moment to micro-manage the whole affair—having second thoughts about the menu or wanting to add games to the program. On the other hand, if he was to decide right now to call the whole thing off, it wouldn't hurt her feelings in the least.

She didn't look at him but concentrated on the silver bells and ribbons on the centerpiece she was putting into place. "If there's something you don't like," she said, "forget it. It's too late to make changes."

From the corner of her eye she noted that he looked around as if for the first time. "No, everything looks fine. I just came to ask if there's anything I can do to help."

"Last week," Paige said acidly, "yes. Yesterday, yes. Today—just stay out of my way."

"How about afterward?"

"After the party?" She eyed him narrowly. "If you wouldn't mind being a bit more specific about what you have in mind—"

Austin's voice was wry. "I was just asking if you need help with the mess afterwards. You needn't fret about hidden meanings, Paige. You made it quite clear that you have no intention of making time for that little chat I asked for."

Sanity reasserted itself. After all, Austin wasn't a fool. He knew there was no point in insisting on another talk when it would change nothing.

It was completely beside the point that something deep inside her wanted him to insist.

"There won't be any mess afterward," she said briskly. "The party cleanup's already arranged. I'll have to stick around to supervise till the bitter end, but there isn't a thing for anyone else to do. And the moment that's done I'm going home to a tub of bubbles, and I'm not getting out for days."

There, she thought. That should make it clear that she wasn't inviting him to stick around and keep her company, either.

"How very efficient you are," he murmured.

Paige didn't think he meant it as a compliment. "And creative, too," she said sweetly. "Don't you like how I turned your new security desk into a platform for the Christmas tree? Right there in the middle—it's the perfect

place for it. Plus I saved Tanner a bundle of money be
cause by putting it up so high I could get by with a muc
smaller tree and still have the same dramatic effect as a
twenty-five-foot one would have.''

"The guards don't seem to like it too well," Austi
pointed out.

"Too bad. Tell them to stop acting like secret agent
for a change and enjoy the party."

Paige wished she could have obeyed her own orders
But there was too much to do—and in the slack moments
there were too many memories to allow her to relax. She
watched from a distance as Jennifer perched on Santa
Claus' lap, and wondered what she was requesting fo
Christmas. She watched as the child slid down and ran t
her father, and she felt a stab of jealousy at the way Austi
swung her up for a hug, with love showing in every lin
of his body.

I made the only decision I could, she told herself. *I
would have killed me to live with him, loving him and
knowing he doesn't love me.*

But the knowledge was cold comfort indeed.

The last cleanup crew finished their work; the last truck
full of garbage pulled away. In the silent atrium, Paige
made her final inspection, making sure that no scrap o
paper, no punch cup, no crushed ribbon, no strand of tinse
had been left behind.

The Christmas tree had been moved from atop the se
curity desk to the out-of-the-way spot at the bend of the
staircase, where it would stay till the season was finished
A silent guard walked through the atrium and eyed he
with professional suspicion. Paige felt like thumbing he
nose at him.

She put her coat on and pushed through the main en

trance—and stared unbelieving at the empty spot in the parking lot where she'd left her van.

It couldn't be gone, she told herself. No car thief in his right mind would drive off with an aging minivan, when there were far more interesting and valuable means of transportation available. But it had without question vanished.

The door opened behind her, and—grateful she hadn't given in to the urge to make faces at the security guard—she turned around to ask for help.

Austin said, "You were right about the cleanup crews you hired. The place looks better than it has since I got here."

Paige blinked. "I thought you left a long time ago."

"I had some work to do, so Cassie took Jennifer home with her. It didn't take much enticement," he added dryly, "because I understand Jake just got himself a dog. I thought you were going home to a tub of bubbles as soon as you'd finished."

"I can't," Paige said bitterly. "My van's been stolen."

Austin's eyebrows arched. "From Tanner's parking lot? Surely not."

"So much for your celebrated security people."

"I'll bet that's the answer. Did you ever get visitor tags for your van?"

Paige's jaw dropped. "Visitor—you have got to be kidding."

Austin nodded. "I'll bet Security towed it. No proper tags. No employee number."

"Damn your security system! They did it to get even with me for the Christmas tree, didn't they?"

"Well, you did put the tree smack in their way," Austin said reasonably. "Can I give you a ride?"

"You can get your bruisers to give my van back."

"If it's in a lockup somewhere, it's probably stuck there till Monday morning. But I'll drive you home."

"You can take me to a rental agency." Paige added sweetly, "And you'll be paying the bill."

"Fair enough. But on a weekend we'd better call first, or you'll end up with a compact that your mother couldn't get into."

Muttering, Paige dug into her tote bag for her cell phone. "You wouldn't happen to know the number?"

Austin complained, "It's too cold to stand out here, anyway. Let's go into the building, at least."

Against her better judgment, she let him take her arm. Inside, she went straight to the security desk. The guard had vanished, no doubt gone to do his regular rounds. But if she could reach a telephone directory...

"When I proposed to you," Austin said quietly, "I meant every word of it, Paige."

"How flattering." She could see the book she needed, but it was just out of reach.

"I was telling you the truth. I believed what I was saying. And I was absolutely wrong."

"That's nice. Can you reach that directory for me?"

"I could, but I won't. Half an hour, Paige, I swear. That's all. Give me half an hour, and then I'll take you home, or call a cab, or do whatever you want."

"And I suppose you'll never mention the subject again?"

"I didn't go quite that far," he admitted.

She turned her back to the security desk and boosted herself up to sit on it. "You're like Chinese water torture, Austin, you know that? You never give up. All right, you've got your half hour." She stretched as far as she could and got her fingertips on the directory.

"The real reason I proposed to you—the reason that I

didn't want to admit even to myself—is because I love you, Paige."

The hand she was using to support herself skidded on the slick surface of the desk, and Austin's iron grip was the only thing that kept Paige from going face-first over the edge.

Austin pulled her back into a sitting position, but he didn't remove his arm from around her waist. Instead he stepped closer, until their faces—on a level because of her perch—were just inches apart.

"Leaving you behind when I left Denver was the single worst decision of my entire life. The stupidest thing I have ever done. Not only do I love you, Paige..." His voice dropped to a husky whisper. "I've never stopped loving you."

Furious, Paige shoved at his chest. He didn't move. "You expect me to believe that? You married Marliss Howard. You have a child—"

"Actually," Austin said, "I didn't."

"What are you talking about? Jennifer is not a figment of my imagination!"

"I mean, I didn't marry her mother."

Paige almost shrieked, "And that's supposed to make me feel better? That you didn't even marry the mother of your child?"

"Well...yes, I expect so. Marliss was a good friend—"

"Yeah," Paige muttered. "I'd say. Now if you don't mind..." She tried to slide off the desk.

Austin held her. "You promised me a half hour."

"Justifying this would take days, Austin. If you think you can do it in your remaining twenty minutes, you're delusional."

"Just let me tell you what happened."

Paige saw the determination in his face and gave up.

She shrugged out of her coat. "I might as well be comfortable."

"I met Marliss when I applied for the Philadelphia job."

"The one you left me for." She was deliberately picking at the wound, making sure she didn't forget how much it had hurt.

He nodded. "She was the human resources manager who interviewed me. I was new in town, and I was just beginning to realize that I'd messed up in a big way. And she was feeling a bit lonely at the time, too."

"Austin, if you fell for that old trick—"

"I'm not defending, just explaining. Marliss's job was choosing people, but in her personal life she apparently didn't apply all the same rules—so when she broke the news to her boyfriend that she was pregnant, he vanished from the picture."

"And of course she needed a friend," Paige said. She didn't even try to keep the sarcasm out of her voice.

Austin didn't seem to hear it. "And then things got worse. When Marliss was four months pregnant, she was diagnosed with ovarian cancer. They couldn't treat it while she was pregnant, and they didn't have time to wait till they could safely deliver the baby. Her only chance to live was to abort the pregnancy."

Paige put her hands over her face. She could almost feel what was coming.

"Marliss refused to do that. If she sacrificed her child, she said, she wouldn't want to live. But she didn't have any illusions about the choice she was making. She asked me—as a friend—to raise her child."

"Jennifer?" Paige whispered.

"I swore to her that I would do my best. I brought Jennifer home from the hospital, and just three weeks later her mother died. The only thing she'd had time to do was sketch out the nursery she wanted her baby to have.''

"Jennifer's room," Paige said. "That's why it was so important to have it right—to make it as close as possible to what her mother planned."

Austin nodded. "It's the only thing she has from Marliss—that and an album of photographs. As soon as the paperwork could be done, I adopted her."

"Does Jennifer know?"

"Yes, though I edited it down to what she can handle, at her age." He sighed. "She saved me, Paige—Jennifer did. And she also forced me to face what I'd done. What I'd given up when I lost you."

She said levelly, "You mean, when you threw me away."

"That hurts—but as you told me once, the truth often does. I was stupid, Paige. I had no idea what I was giving up when I left you. I put my ambition above my commitment to you—told myself that the desire to succeed was natural and normal, that I was only trying to provide well for you, and that if you really loved me you'd see that. I convinced myself you were just being selfish."

"Trying to keep you from chasing the brass ring."

"By the time I realized that there were more important things than getting to the top of a corporate mountain, it was too late to patch the mistake. So I went on. I did the best I could to juggle my job and my daughter. And I pretended I didn't miss you."

She sighed. "Why did you come back to Denver, Austin?"

He said wryly, "I thought it was because Caleb offered me a terrific opportunity—a job I would love but which was flexible enough to let me make up for the time I'd missed with Jennifer."

"And the first person you run into is me. That must have been quite a surprise."

"Not really," he admitted. "I saw our china at Sabrina's dinner party the night of my interview—the china you'd picked out as our wedding pattern even though we didn't have a table to put it on. And it didn't take much inquiry to find out there was an elusive third partner in Rent-A-Wife and her name was Paige."

"That's what you meant," she said, startled. "When you first came into the apartment and I was there, you said, 'It *was* you.' You sounded so strange—almost as if you were relieved, and yet I didn't think that was possible."

"Relieved? Yes, but I was still too proud to admit it. I didn't know I was coming back here to find you, Paige. I just knew I wanted to come home. I wanted to set down roots. I wanted to build a family. It wasn't until I saw you with Jennifer that I realized I wanted to build that family with you. I even told your mother the day I came to pick Jennifer up that I was back to stay—but I was still too proud to admit the reason."

Paige could hardly take it in, herself. He'd told Eileen? No wonder her mother had looked as if she'd had an electrical shock.

"You'd gone on without me," he said softly, "and it hurt. That was why I let you believe that I'd married Marliss, that I went straight from you to another woman. You didn't seem to miss me in the least. And I thought the only thing I could offer you, the only thing that might tempt you—"

"Was money," she said softly. "The very thing that took you away from me in the first place."

"I'm a fool, Paige. A blind, stupid fool, not to know what was happening to me. I wouldn't blame you a bit if you told me to get lost." His voice was husky.

She smiled a little. "Why bother? You wouldn't do it."

Austin's jaw tightened. "If that's what you want, Paige—"

She shook her head, and watched the slow dawn of hope in his eyes. The glow of it took her breath away, and she had to swallow hard before she could speak. "I want to be Paige Weaver again," she said softly.

He swept her down from the security desk and into his arms, and for a long time Paige's world narrowed till there was room for only the two of them.

Finally, when he stopped kissing her, she admitted with a tremor in her voice, "I wanted so much to say yes. But I didn't think it was me you really wanted. I thought you were looking for a symbol, and an errand-runner, and a nanny—"

"Shall I prove it's you I want?" he asked. "I always did like a good challenge."

She held him off. "Let me finish. You were right when you said I was selfish not to go with you, Austin. Yes, my mother needed me right then—but that's not why I stayed. Even then, you'd changed from when we were first married. You were growing distant. The new job wasn't going to be any different, really, except that it would be even worse. Longer hours, more things to prove. Less time for me." She took a deep breath. "If I'd been convinced I was important to you, I could have fought. But I thought I didn't matter to you. And if I wasn't going to have a marriage, anyway, then I might as well be here, where my mother needed me. Where *somebody* needed me."

"I need you," he whispered. "Not to be a symbol. Not to smooth my life. Not to be a nanny. I need *you*, Paige— my wife, my lover, my love. I should never have left you—"

She laid a finger across his lips to silence him. "If you

hadn't,'' she reminded softly, "we wouldn't have Jennifer.''

"*We?* You don't know how happy that makes me. My darling, I've never stopped loving you. But I've also never loved you as much as I do right now.''

It was a long time later that Paige tugged playfully at his earlobe and said, ''I hate to be practical, but it's getting late and I still need a car. Just because Ben Orcutt seems to be spending the better part of his waking hours at my house these days doesn't mean I can depend on him for transportation.''

''Is he really?''

''Today he brought popcorn and a movie, and when I was leaving I heard Mother laugh. I thought she'd forgotten how.'' She swallowed hard. ''So go ahead and say you told me so.''

Austin shook his head. ''I wouldn't dream of it. I was jealous of Eileen, too—but now I'm glad that she'll always need you. Maybe it will just be in different ways.''

Paige blinked back tears. ''About that rental car—''

''You don't need one.''

''Why? You're going to stick around all weekend and be a taxi service?'' The idea had its positive aspects, she decided.

''If you like. But your van should be in your driveway by now. Right where I told the tow truck driver to take it.''

She stared at him. ''*You* had my van towed? And then you blamed security for it?''

''Well,'' he said reasonably, ''I had to get my half hour somehow. Do you really think it was such a bad idea?''

She smiled, and shook her head. ''Caleb was absolutely right. Whatever Austin wants, Austin gets.''

''And,'' he whispered, holding her even closer, ''Austin keeps.''

If you enjoyed what you just read,
then we've got an offer you can't resist!

Take 2 bestselling
love stories FREE!
Plus get a FREE surprise gift!

Coming in June from

HARLEQUIN
AMERICAN ◆ ROMANCE®

MAITLAND MATERNITY

When two sets
of twins are born at
Maitland Maternity Hospital on
the same day, unforgettable surprises
are sure to follow. Don't miss the fun, the
romance, the joy...as two special couples find
love just outside the delivery room door.

Watch for:
SURPRISE! SURPRISE!
by Tina Leonard
On sale June 2000.

I DO! I DO!
by Jacqueline Diamond
On sale July 2000.

And there will be many more Maitland Maternity
stories when a special twelve-book continuity series
launches in August 2000.
Don't miss any of these stories by wonderful
authors such as Marie Ferrarella, Jule McBride,
Muriel Jensen and Judy Christenberry.

Available at your favorite retail outlet.

HARLEQUIN®
Makes any time special ™

Visit us at www.eHarlequin.com.

HARMMDD

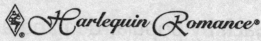

Romance is just one click away!

online book **serials**

- *Exclusive* to our web site, get caught up in both the daily and weekly online installments of new romance stories.
- Try the Writing Round Robin. Contribute a chapter to a story created by our members. Plus, winners will get prizes.

romantic **travel**

- Want to know where the best place to kiss in New York City is, or which restaurant in Los Angeles is the most romantic? Check out our Romantic Hot Spots for the scoop.
- Share your travel tips and stories with us on the romantic travel message boards.

romantic reading **library**

- Relax as you read our collection of Romantic Poetry.
- Take a peek at the Top 10 Most Romantic Lines!

Visit us online at

www.eHarlequin.com
on Women.com Networks

HARLEQUIN®
Romance®

Margot, *Shelby* and *Georgia*
are getting married. But first they have
a mystery to solve....

Join these three sisters on the way to the
altar in an exciting new trilogy from

BARBARA McMAHON

in Harlequin Romance

MARRYING MARGOT July 2000

A MOTHER FOR MOLLIE August 2000

GEORGIA'S GROOM September 2000

**Three sisters uncover secrets—
that lead to marriage with
the men of their dreams!**

HARLEQUIN®
Makes any time special ™